Love Me, Stevie C.

MICHELLE GAYLE'S career has spanned TV, theatre, film and music. She was first known for her TV appearances, which began in the 1980s with children's drama *Grange Hill*, followed by *EastEnders*, before she moved over to a glittering pop career that saw her achieve six top twenty hits and sell a million records, most successfully her 1994 single "Sweetness". Michelle has since appeared on TV shows such as *Doctors*, *Holby City* and *Family Affairs*, and she starred opposite Ed Stoppard in the 2006 film *Joy Division*. In recent years Michelle has presented on *Loose Women* and also taken part in reality TV shows *Come Dine with Me* and *Dancing on Wheels*. Michelle lives with her husband and two sons in west London.

So-ooo, THE story so far...

Me, Remy Louise Bennet? Check!
One hot bloke? Check!
Football? Ugh! Check!
Gossip? Check!
Drama? Double-check!
Want more juicy details?

Don't Lie To Me, Robbie Wilkins
is available from all great booksellers.

Check it out!

Tee-hee!
Love
Remy x x x ☺

Say You Love Me, Stevie C.

MICHELLE GAYLE

**WALKER
BOOKS**

First published 2013 by Walker Books Ltd
87 Vauxhall Walk, London SE11 5HJ

2 4 6 8 10 9 7 5 3 1

Text © 2013 Michelle Gayle
Cover and inside illustrations © 2013 Paula Castro
Cover design by Walker Books Ltd

This book has been typeset in Fairfield

Printed and bound in Great Britain by Clays Ltd, St Ives plc

British Library Cataloguing in Publication Data:
a catalogue record for this book is available from the British Library

ISBN 978-1-4063-3929-1

www.walker.co.uk

For Tony, Isaiah and Luke

SALON IDOL

COURTNEY

MON: 3 WAXES, 3 MANICURES — 6 pts
1 man/ped. — 2 pts
STAY LATE BONUS 1 pt = 9 pts

TUES: IN BEFORE 8.45 — 1 pt
1 MAN, 1 MAN/PED 1 WAX = 4 pts.
"FABULICIOUS" HAIR BONUS: 1 pt.

TOTAL SO FAR: (15)

LARA

MON: 4 WAXES 1 MANICURE — 5 pts
1 MAN/PED = 2 pts
2 CLIENTS BOUGHT PRODUCTS 2 pts = 9 pts

TUES: IN BEFORE 8.45 — 1 pt
2 WAXES, 1 MAN/PED = 4 pts

TOTAL SO FAR: (14)

still!

Remy + Leonardo DiCaprio 4ever! ☺

Shia La"Buff"
– Phwoar!!

Tinie Tempah
– Hot!!

TAH★DAH
50%

Saturday 21 February — 7.45 a.m.

I, Remy Louise Bennet, solemnly swear not to neglect this diary any more. Been slack for the past three weeks for two reasons:

1. Am now a big bossy-ish salon owner.
2. Been busy building romantico relationship with fit new Scottish boyfriend.

And, apart from an ickle disagreement last night, it's going quite well. In fact, ready for work and staring at a sleeping McFitness right now. ☺

Eek! He's just opened his eyes and caught me gawping at him. Hope he doesn't think I'm a bunny-boiler. Will smile, non-psycho-like, and make out that I spotted a fly buzzing around his face…

Methinks I got away with it by swatting said imaginary fly with my hands.

"It can nae kill me," he said. "Now give me a goodbye kiss before I jump in the shower."

Anytime! I thought. And could there be more perfect lips? Just about managed to pull away from them to say, "See you tomorrow."

"Kick-off's at four tomorrow, Boss Lady, and the coach ride from Newcastle takes ages, so it'll be too late for us to meet up by the time I get back. We'll have to leave it till Monday."

Oh no—ooooooooooo! Being without him tonight was bad enough but tomorrow as well just proves what I've always believed: football sucks. Although, must admit there are perks: Netherfield Park Rangers paying for Stephen to stay in this swanky hotel in the Docklands, for instance.

"Unless…" He sighed.

"Unless what?"

"Yer fancy the train ride up there? Then you'll finally get to see me play. *Live.*"

"But I *will* be seeing you play live."

He frowned.

"On Sky Sports," I explained, straight-faced.

"Oh … yeah … but…" he stammered, ever Mr Polite. I couldn't resist smiling. "Are you winding me up?" he checked.

"Of course I am. I'm not *that* thick."

He laughed. "Just think a Sunday game will be perfect for you, cos you don't have to work."

Yep, he's right. My "too busy working at the salon" excuse definitely won't cut it this time.

"My parents and Angus will be there if yer worried about being on your own."

A chance to meet his family and best friend too – now that's BIG. Maybe even the extra kick up the bum I need to walk into the players' lounge and finally deal with being in the same room as my twot-faced ex: Stephen's teammate, Robbie Wilkins. And I will be strong. I will remind the little git that I'm not a gold-digging WAG wannabe like he told Stephen, but a v. ambitious salon mogul. Yeah! Do it, Remy.

"I'll be there," I told him. "Um... Just as long as there are no hiccups at the salon today." #ColdFeet ☹

"Right, better get off to work, Boss Lady. Can't be late and all that."

7.40 p.m.

I'm home. And not knackered but *ker*-knackered (more extreme, near-death level form of tiredness). Had my first horrible customer today. It was in the morning too (not my best time) and it took all my blooming energy to deal with her without use of swear words, or physical abuse. Now OK, something did go wrong with the Tanarama booth settings. And, yes, she did step out of it looking like an Oompa-Loompa, but I apologized close to two thousand times and that still wasn't good enough.

"Look at me, my skin's ruined!"

My ex-boss (and owner of Kara's, the salon down the road) used to do my head in – which is why she deserved to be called the Feminazi. But now I at least admire the way she used to deal with unhappy customers. She'd turn on the poshness and say some proper long words that confused people until they just mumbled, "OK," when she offered a free beauty product as compensation. I decided to try that. How hard could it be?

"Don't worry, Miss Weeks. Your skin will be *absolutely*, *fantastically* fine after a few scrubs. And please bear in mind that *technically*, with it being an *automated* spray-tan booth, it isn't actually my fault. However, please take a moisturizer or a nail varnish of your choice to make up for it."

"Is that all?!"

"Um… And I'd also like to offer two Tanarama sessions once the booth is fixed – free of charge of course."

"And a manicure an' all, yeah?" she demanded.

Why oh why do they have that stupid rule that says the customer's always right?

I visualized myself in a parallel universe where it was OK to put my hands around her bright orange neck and squee–eeeze. BLISS.

"Sure, Miss Weeks—"

"Mrs," she corrected.

"*Mrs* Weeks. I'll throw in a Tah-dah! Magic Manicure as well," I told her, which just happens to be the most expensive one.

Grrr.

Now just want to put on some PJs, chill out on the sofa and veg in front of *Keeping Up with the Kardashians*.

7.45 P.M.

Eww! Went to the living room to watch TV, but Mum and Alan were wrapped around each other on the sofa. Think this is highly insensitive considering they know I'm in the house. Yes, I've moved back in and I do talk to them (to be polite), but that doesn't mean I'm over them STABBING DAD IN THE BACK. Besides, they're too old to be acting like that.

Mum asked if I'd spoken to Malibu today and then when I said I hadn't she went off on one about me needing to be a supportive sister. Wanted to tell her that Dad needs support too. It can't be easy adjusting to not seeing us every day. Mum didn't give me a chance though: she was still going on about helping Malibu out.

"You wait till the baby's here. *That's* when the real problems start," she finished.

Why did she emphasize the "that"? I wondered. *Does she know? But surely Malibu wouldn't have told her.* I decided it was best to be cautious. "Why? What did she say?"

"That she's scared. And she sounded it too. *Very.*"

Hmm. Scared about giving birth or ... the results of giving birth, so to speak? As in the baby not looking like the dad it's supposed to look like? Couldn't decide. And yes, I may have blurted out every secret ever told to me, but not this time. No. Way.

"Yeah, OK. I'll call her now," I said to play safe. Then I got out of there, pronto – before they both got lovey-dovey again.

7.50 P.M.

Bloody Nora! Train tickets to Newcastle have gone up sixty pounds since the last time I looked. Would now cost two hundred and twenty quid – could buy two Sneezy-Jet tix to Magaluf for that! Don't think I can afford it.

8 P.M.

"You're just making an excuse," snapped Malibu. Called her to "offer support" but she asked what I was up to, and when I told her about the ticket predicament, she ended up giving me a lecture. Typical. ☺ "You should make the effort. And even more important than that is him *seeing* that you have because, no offence, I don't think you went all out for Robbie. And if you don't make a man feel special, Remy, there are hundreds of other women that will."

Gr–rreat. My big sis was now hinting that it was *my* fault Robbie did the dirty on me. Would normally have dug in and argued with her but the phone call wasn't meant to be about my problems (which happen to be teeny compared with hers).

"OK, OK. How are you, anyway? Mum said I should call."

She sighed. "Not good."

"Why, what's happened?"

Had Gary "Goldenballs" discovered that the baby might actually be Lance Wilson's? Or was the guilt of keeping such a big secret getting to her, causing sleepless nights, panic attacks, stress? No.

"I need a vajazzle," Malibu said.

"A *what*?"

"A VJ. I can't tell you how ugly I feel carrying around an extra stone and a half. So I thought I'd pop into yours and pamper myself by snazzing up downstairs."

"No way," I told her.

"Why?"

I pointed out that she was almost eight months pregnant, so would be v. inappropriate.

And she said that I was living in the Dark Ages and I'd be surprised by what pregnant women got up to nowadays.

A majorly gross image of her and Goldenballs flashed into my head. *Surely they can't still be at it – not in her condition?*

"I'm gonna be sick in my mouth now," I told her. But she still didn't change the subject.

"I went to watch Gary play today, and the girls were

saying that you can't afford to let yourself go – even when you're pregnant. The WAG wannabes are actually more dangerous then."

"Yeah, well somehow I don't think they mean you need to decorate your privates with crystals."

"Come on, Rem. Gary's so good to me – I just want to repay him with a nice surprise. Ple–eeeeeease. You owe me anyway."

"For?"

"Neglect."

She had a point. Have been a pretty useless sister these past three weeks since the salon opened.

"And it's my birthday next week. You can make it an early prezzie."

Mal's twenty-five on 1 March.

"Pretty purlease?"

"Oh … OK then. I'll *think* about it," I groaned.

"Perfect. Speak tomorrow. Oh, and Rem?"

"Yes?"

"Check out the Zoe Westwick column in *Hey There!*"

"*Who?*"

"Zoe Westwick – the relationship guru. I think you could do with some tips."

Oh, the irony. ☹

<u>8.05 P.M.</u>

Newcastle… Still can't decide whether to go or not.

16

Reasons to go:

  1. Will meet Stephen's parents.

  2. Will meet his best friend Angus.

  3. Making such a big effort will probably squash any bad feelings about our ickle argument last night.

Such a stupid argument too. All because I accused him of looking at a barmaid's bum.

"She's got a Post-it note on it that says 'private property'," he'd explained.

Instead of checking whether it was true, I'd snapped, "Well that *proves* you were looking at her bum."

"Boss Lady, I think you need an ice-cold can of Chill-ade."

Trust issues – yet another thing I can blame Robbie Wilkins for. ☹

Reasons not to go:

  1. Robbie – OF COURSE.

Thing is, not only will I have to deal with Robbie – I reckon my name's dirt with most of the people at Netherfield Park now, especially with the WAGs. They can be right bitches.

Oh no, I can hear Mum and Alan giggling. Eww! Now Mum's telling him to stop because she's ticklish!

Dear God, please let me win the lottery so I can buy a house and move out!

"Come on, baby-wayby, you know you love it!"

Ugh! That's it. Phoning my besties to see if they're free tonight – have to escape the Born-Again Teenagers. Pronto!

<u>8.10 P.M.</u>

Called Kellie but she's going to the cinema with her boy-friend, Jack. She said I could come too but they're worse than the Born-Again Teenagers, and without Stephen I'd feel v. awkward. Will now phone James.

<u>8.15 P.M.</u>

"Hello–oo, what you doing tonight?" I asked James.

"Hey hon. One of my workmates is having a party. It's going to be fierce."

"Where?"

"Shoreditch."

"Can I come?"

"I take it Stephen isn't around then," he replied in a sarky tone.

"Um … no, he isn't actually. Had to go to Newcastle for the game tomorrow. Why?"

"Because you wouldn't be wanting to come out if he was."

"Oi! Don't begrudge me the honeymoon period. Besides, I haven't been that bad."

"No. You've been worse than bad. But it's OK. I'll still be here to pick up the pieces."

James has been working at Cutz hair salon in Shoreditch for two weeks and they seem to be adding bitchiness to his wage packet.

"The pieces?! There won't be any *pieces* – he's nothing like Robbie."

"We hope."

Grrr.

"Look, can I come to the party – yes or no?"

"Of course you can. Then you can meet Rupert." His voice definitely lifted.

"Oooh, who's Rupert?"

"My new boyfriend. He just doesn't know it yet. In fact, I'm pretty sure he doesn't know I exist!" We both laughed.

"And what does Rupert do then?"

"That's the best bit – he works at Villa House."

I have no idea what Villa House is so I just said, "Wow. Cool. See you later."

8.20 p.m.

It'll be hard to talk properly once I'm out with James, so thought I'd better phone Stephen and make a decision.

"Hey Boss Lady, I was just about to call you."

"Aha! Great minds think alike."

"Aye. They do. Now, are yer coming to Newcastle?"

"Um…"

"It's OK if yer can't. I mean I want yer to but … I don't want yer to feel pressurized."

"Oh no. It's no pressure," I pretended.

"Good. Because if you can't come, Angus will use your ticket to bring his sister – but only if yer can't make it."

Sister? Aka another woman willing to fill my shoes, just like Malibu predicted. "You've never mentioned that Angus has a sister."

"Aye. He has two."

Gr–rreat. What was he going to say next: "And they're both beautiful"?!

"And do both sisters want to go?"

"No. Just Beth."

"Oh. *Be–eeth*."

"Aye. She's the younger one."

Well, hopefully that means she's sixty-three, I thought. "Really? How old is she?"

"Twelve."

Yippee! Twelve equals no threat, and no threat equals no need for me to go to Newcastle, and no need to see Robbie and the WAGs!

"Ahhh. Twelve," I gushed.

"Aye. She's a sweet wee thing."

"Yes. Well… In that case, she's probably really looking forward to it. And I'd feel bad if she missed out, so…" I sighed. "Let her go instead."

"You sure?" Stephen sounded surprised. "I thought you really wanted to come."

"Oh, I do! But … I'd feel terrible knowing I'd spoilt Beth's chance to go. Especially when I can see your next game."

"Oh." He sounded surprised again. "Aren't Saturdays still a problem?"

"Saturdays? Yes. Of course. Big problem. Well, they have been up until now, that is, but the beauticians are settling in well, so I'm sure I'll be able to leave the salon in their hands... Soon... In the very near future."

"Right."

He sounded disappointed. Feel bad now. ☹

9.05 p.m.

Oh yes—ss, methinks James will be v. impressed when he sees me. Tonight I'm rocking the sexy-chic look and I copied almost everything *Flair* mag said: tight, sparkly dress. Check! (Mine has gold sequins.) High-heeled pumps. Check! (Also gold.) Stylish accessories. Check! (Chain-mail earrings bought using Topshop staff discount – thank you, Kel!) Glamorous hair. Double-check! (Hot-brushed and big and bouncy – like Cheryl Cole in that ad.)

Shoreditch, here I come!

3 a.m.

I blooming hate Shoreditch! AND James has proper pissed me off tonight. He should have told me that place isn't for normal people like me. It's for arty-farty types. Attention-seekers. Knobheads (in Rupert's case). I swear Lady Gaga could walk down Shoreditch High Street in her meat dress and nobody would bat an eyelid.

Should have realized something was wrong as soon as James opened his front door. He usually compliments my clothes or hair, so I thought he'd be all over my sexy-chic look. But all he did was groan, "What took you so long?"

Another clue was what he was wearing. He's kissed goodbye to Hollister T-shirts and loose-fit Levi's; and said hello to skinny jeans, patent shoes, a black bowtie (v. random) and a brown leather jacket that looked like it'd gone ten rounds with David Haye. Even worse, it was throwing out one hell of a pong – not a sweaty one but an old "been in a dusty cupboard for ten years" type of smell. WTF?!

Didn't want to hurt his feelings when he asked whether I liked it so I just mumbled, "Yeah."

"Thanks. It's vintage," he replied, looking pleased with himself.

Yeah, I smelt that. "Great," I said.

But then he still didn't mention my sexy-chic look. ☹

When the bus hit Shoreditch High Street, I realized why.

"*What* is he wearing?" I pointed at a guy in a multi-coloured jumpsuit, thinking James would laugh.

"I think he looks fab. It's all about individuality in Shoreditch. Trying to reflect your personality instead of following whatever style *Flair* says you should be wearing this week."

Ouch.

"But you used to love *Flair*," I told him.

"Yeah," he replied. "And then I grew up."

See what I mean about the bitchiness?

The bar was called Chill Zone and by the time we got there, we'd passed enough "individuals" to make me realize that my outfit was a huge mistake.

"Why didn't you say?" I complained to James. "I feel so out of place."

"We were running late as it was. Besides, it's not like you could have gone home, changed and made it better. You don't have anything—" He stopped himself.

"Anything what?" I pressed.

"Anything 'Shoreditch' anyway."

No. Nothing "Sho–ooreditch". Not like Rainbow, the girl in charge of the guestlist, who was wearing enormous fake eyelashes, a Sixties-style mini dress and a white fur cape. If we'd been anywhere else, I would have thought she was in fancy dress. Austin Powers' assistant maybe?

"What a fabulous outfit, dahling," James told her, over-pronouncing his words like he was talking to a nan who's hard of hearing.

"Thanks," Rainbow replied. "It's vintage."

I just about managed to stop myself from pointing out, "What you REALLY mean is *second-hand*."

Inside, Chill Zone was packed with Shoreditch types rocking the Shoreditch look, and Rupert was no exception. He was wearing green skinny jeans, a checked shirt, purple Dr. Martens and exactly the same leather jacket that James had on.

"Hello dahling," he said to James. Then he frowned at me as though I were some kind of alien species – a "big-haired sequin" maybe? – before pecking James on both cheeks. *Mwah, mwah.*

"This is Rupert," James announced with a big grin. "And you're going to get us into Villa House – aren't you, Rupert?"

"If you play your cards right," Rupert flirted back.

"And this is Remy. You know, the friend I told you I used to go to college with."

Rupert gave me a David Attenborough look again – like he was thinking, *Is she even from this planet?*

"Did James do your hair?" he asked when he'd finished his inspection.

"No. No, she did it herself," James quickly cut in.

Rupert's nose creased like a dog had laid one on his top lip. "Thought as much," he said, then walked off.

Didn't want it to bother me, but five minutes later I went to the toilet and patted my hair down – at least then it was only ten centimetres bigger than everyone else's. Couldn't find James when I came back. He'd gone off to the toilets with Rupert and they both came back with saucepan-sized pupils, giggling. *roll eyes*

Thankfully, Rupert kept his distance after that. He was Mr Popular, flitting between different groups. James stayed with me, in body anyway, but his eyes always followed Rupert everywhere. It got on my nerves at first – made me wonder whether he regretted bringing me. But it's surprising how little things matter after a few mojitos (definitely my new favourite drink)! And I can handle it as well. Only feel a teensy-weensy bit tipsy and I must have had at least six of them. ☺

Sunday 22 February – 9.25 a.m.

Ughhhh! My head! And why am I lying in bed fully clothed, with a face full of make-up? What a skank!

9.30 a.m.

Need aspirin, paracetamol, tranquillizers, ibuprofen, ANY-THING. Kitchen cupboard – BE PREPARED.

9.35 a.m.

"Gordon Bennet, looks like someone had a good night, buddy," Alan joked when I staggered into the kitchen. All those years in Australia means that he constantly slips from an Aussie to a Cockney accent in one sentence. It makes me smile but only on the inside – no way am I going to let him see the corners of my mouth turned up.

"Fancy some bacon and eggs?" he asked.

Boy, would I have killed for some bacon and eggs.

"No thanks," I groaned because my loyalty remains with Dad. (Just wish Alan would stop trying to be so flipping nice.)

Right, downed two Nurofen, now clothes off and back to bed. Yippee!

Methinks the bloke that came up with ibuprofen should be knighted. Headache is completely gone. Yay!

Only problem is, I'm wide a-blooming-wake now. Boo!

Aha! Brought the sales ledger home from the salon. Will get the maths out of the way and add up the weekly takings. (Worst part of the job.)

I'm on a timeout. When God handed out the maths brains, methinks I was hibernating. It's beyond hard – even with a calculator. Just going to check my Facebook page for a second and chill out. Fifteen/twenty minutes tops.

I wonder what Stephen's up to? I wonder whether he's wondering about me? Hope so.

Would be great if he was lying in bed thinking, *Remy's so–oo awesome.* ☺

Thing about Stephen is, he stimulates me in every department. Spencer was a great friend-type boyfriend and Robbie was a sexy one (as well as a liar and a cheat). But

Stephen has all their good points and more. Can't imagine how I'd have got through these first three weeks of running the salon without him there, insisting that my hard work would pay off eventually. Whatta dude.

Right, suppose I'd better get back to the sales ledger.

10.55 a.m.

Got distracted again, this time by a phone call from Kel.

"What'd you end up doing last night?" she asked.

"Went to a party with James."

"Any good?"

"An epic let-down," I said. "Have you ever gone out in Shoreditch?"

"No."

"Well, don't. It's not very us. How was the film?"

"Boring. *Except* that I bumped into Lance Wilson and Amy 'local bike' Fitzgerald."

"No way."

"Yep. In the popcorn queue. And when she went to the toilet, he asked how you and Malibu were doing."

"You didn't tell him she was pregnant, did you?"

"Nah. I just told him you're both fine and that your salon's smashing it. He looked hot though – if you like that kind of thing. Which I don't of course."

Kellie's never gone out with a blond guy. Her type is tall and dark, though she does say that she'd make an exception for Ryan Gosling.

"So, was that guy James keeps going on about there?"

"Who, Rupert?"

"Yeah. What's he like?"

"We need a whole day to talk about *him*. And I need to get on with the sales ledger."

"Cool. Catch you later then," she said.

11.05 a.m.

Still haven't gone back to the ledger. Kellie asking about Rupert made me call James instead. Didn't want to give her the full deets until I'd had it out with him. He was a naughty boy last night, and I've been giving him some time to sleep it off. When he answered the phone, he sounded worse than I'd felt this morning.

"Ugh. What time is it?"

"Eleven."

"Call me back in about two hours."

"No."

"What?"

"No."

"Why not?"

"Because I'm not stupid, James. I know you took drugs when you went to the toilets last night," I snapped.

"So?"

"So, I want to talk about it."

"Oh, here we go," he groaned. "A lecture from Little Miss Perfect."

"Whatever. But you're the one who said you'd never do drugs after Lucy Parker almost died."

"That was ecstasy. I took pure MDMA. Rupert says that's much safer."

"Oh, it's OK now Rupert says so, is it? Even though you made me swear not to take anything. We both did."

"We were kids then."

"It was ten months ago."

"Yes, well *four* months ago you were blubbing on my shoulder, swearing that you'd never go near another footballer. Now look at you. Still sure you're not a gold-digger?"

Couldn't believe he could say something that spiteful.

"I expect that from those bitches at Netherfield Park. Not you, James."

"I'm sorry," he said. "But I did ask you to call me back in two hours. I'll be more myself then."

"Well, let's hope so cos, for the record, Rupert – or whatever it was you took – has turned you into a right twot."

11.40 a.m.

I'm www.starving.com so I was gutted to see Mum finishing the last bit of bacon when I walked into the kitchen.

"Sorry, dear. Alan said you didn't want any. Didn't you, my loverly man?" She planted a big kiss on his mouth. Eww!

"Fine. I'll just *starve* then," I told her and came back to my room.

Those two do my head in. When I get old, I wouldn't mind being as loved-up with Stephen as they are, but I'll definitely make sure we don't overdo it and gross out our children.

Actually called him a few minutes ago to wish him good luck with his game.

"Hi gorgeous, was just thinking about you. Are you psychic?" he asked when he answered.

"Hopefully. And today, I predict that Stephen Campbell will score loads of goals."

"Do yer now? That would be good, but it'd be even better if you were here to see me score them."

"If only," I told him, and a part of me wished I'd been brave enough to face Robbie. "What did you do last night?"

"Nothing much. Played a bit of poker with Tommy and Darren."

"Did you win?"

"Let's just say they were relieved when I handed all their money back at the end of the night."

"Ahh. You're all heart."

"Aye. That's my trouble."

Defender Tommy Roberts and goalkeeper Darren Hargreaves have gone out of their way to be friendly to Stephen. The others in the squad have kept their distance. And Terry Dawson hasn't said one single word to him. (Kind of understandable, seeing as he's Robbie's best mate.)

Intended to get back to the sales ledger straight after our chat but my brain took a teensy-weensy detour and I've been trying to work out what to call our kids ever since. Ideally, we'll have a boy and a girl, and I reckon Stephen would love them to have traditional Scottish names, so I've Googled some. Can't decide. It's between Ewan and Dougie for our son, and Kirsty and Effie for our daughter.

Eek! Phone's ringing.

11.45 a.m.

It was Malibu.

"Are you on the way to Newcastle?"

"Er… No."

She let out a long and deliberate sigh.

"What?" I said. "His best friend wanted to take his little sister. What was I supposed to do – crush a little girl's dream?"

"You're a wuss."

"I am not a wuss. I am a very considerate person that sacrificed my seat."

"Crap. You were scared."

"No, I wasn't. Well … OK. I admit there might have been a very tiny percentage of me that was slightly nervous about seeing Robbie. But the bigger percentage – the *good* part – was… You're right. I'm a wimp."

"How did he take it?"

"Not bad. Only slightly disappointed."

"We'll talk about it later," she said and invited me to her house for lunch. "Dad's going to come as well. He'll pick you up. And that way we can all watch the Nether-field Park game together."

"Who's cooking?" I asked.

"Me of course."

"You?!" Couldn't believe this was the same Malibu Bennet who'd once burnt boiled eggs.

"I'm doing roast chicken, Jamaican-style – with rice and peas. Gary's mum gave me the recipe. She's coming round to taste it, and I could really do with you backing me up."

I still remember the yummy meal Mrs Johnson cooked for Christmas, and I don't think Malibu will be able to re-create it any time soon. But if she wanted me to back her up – I was going to be there.

Note to self: Must put some indigestion tablets in my bag (just in case).

8 P.M.

Malibu opened her front door and prompted that awkward moment when you realize your heavily pregnant sister still looks better than you: hair – fluffy; face – glowing; and dressed in a floaty chiffon number. I'd thrown on some leggings, a baggy black jumper and my chocolate brown Uggs, and was minus make-up because Dad texted that he was at the top of our road just as I was about to put some on – it's the closest he'll come to the house now that Alan lives with us. ☹ Anyhoo, the rest of the day went downhill from there.

Goldenballs, his mum and his sister, Rochelle, were already in the dining room.

"Sit yourselves down," Malibu said, before adding in a posh Uptown Downstairs Abbey voice, "And lunch will be served."

"Need any help?" asked Mrs Johnson.

"It's OK, Mum – that's what Gary's for."

It was the first time I'd heard her call Mrs Johnson "Mum".

"Yeah, I'm her servant," Gary joked.

"No, babe, don't demean yourself. More my ... assistant." He looked at her and laughed and Malibu's eyes twinkled back as if they were talking in code. "But you can chill out today, honey," she said. "I'll get Remy to help with the salad."

"Me?!" I said. "Don't you want it to be edible?"

"So how's it going with Stephen?" she asked as I diced some spring onions.

"Great," I gushed.

"Is it love?"

Why did she have to bring up the "L" word? I've been avoiding saying it to everybody – including him. Don't want to jinx things by making the same mistakes I made with Robbie – rushing headlong into thinking I'm with "The One", only to end up with a broken heart. But when you're choosing the names of the children you plan to have with somebody, I suppose it can only mean one thing.

"Yeah. I love him," I admitted. "He's amazing."

"But does *he* love *you*? Because that's the most important thing," she said, and immediately made me regret opening up to her.

"Why can't you just let things be? There doesn't always have to be some sort of payback, you know."

"You'll learn," she sighed.

Surprisingly, lunch tasted … OK. Not actually poisonous but it was never going to win *MasterChef* either. The M&S apple pie for dessert was the highlight, and Mrs Johnson stood up to make a speech just as Gary was about to cut it. I crossed my fingers, hoping that it wouldn't take as long … as … last … Christ–mas.

"I would just like to say that … Malibu, we are so glad Gary met you. We have certainly … never seen him so happy. We … cannot wait for the wedding but … you are already my daughter as far as I am concerned so … please phone me if you need any help wit' anyt'ing. Especially … once my grandchild is born."

I was first to clap (relief from how short the speech was, methinks) and everyone else joined in as Mrs Johnson slowly took her seat again. Once the clapping was over, Dad raised his wine glass for a toast: "To the baby," he said. And within seconds, all our glasses were raised and we were chanting, "To the baby!"

Malibu was crying by the time she'd put down her glass.

"You all right, babe?" Gary asked.

"Yes… I'm just so happy," she said.

Dear God, I thought, *please, please, please let Gary be the father of her child.*

Once we'd cleared the plates after dessert, we all sat in the lounge to watch Stephen's match. Malibu told Rochelle and Mrs Johnson that we were excited because my boyfriend plays for Netherfield Park.

"You nervous?" Rochelle asked, as the referee blew his whistle for kick-off.

"Nah. Got a really good feeling about today!"

Couldn't have been more wrong.

I may know nothing about football but when the half-time whistle went, even I realized Dad was right when he said Stephen looked "a bit off the pace". And that was putting it nicely because it looked like it would take a miracle for him to score one goal, let alone the "loads" I'd predicted.

"It's only nil–nil. All to play for," Goldenballs said to me as a consolation. But Stephen kept on losing the ball at the start of the second half and, to make it worse, he was substituted by Robbie in the sixty-third minute. I hadn't expected Gary to stop being friends with Robbie because of our break-up, but it was gutting to hear him clap Robbie on. Malibu, sitting beside him on the sofa, swiftly gave his ribs a sharp dig with her elbow. The applause stopped dead. But I was already cringing. I knew the Netherfield Park WAGs would be having a right old gossip: "Remy's new boyfriend substituted by Remy's ex – oh–hhh my–yyy God!!!" Stupid cows.

"Don't worry," said Dad as Stephen trudged off the pitch. "St James's Park is a hard place to crack."

But I was worried. Some players go into mourning after a bad game. They really beat themselves up and need support from family, friends and loved ones. And there I was, hundreds of miles away at my sister's house. Can't tell you how pissed off with myself that made me. Why, oh why hadn't I gone to Newcastle?

Then, as if the universe wanted me and Stephen to suffer even more, Robbie went on to score in the ninetieth minute, making it Netherfield Park: 1, Newcastle: 0.

It was obviously the winning goal and Robbie ran up to the TV camera and shouted, "I'm the man!" down the lens.

God had clearly run out of modesty by the time he got to Robbie Wilkins.

Anyhoo, no way was I going to let the arrogant twot-face get to me. Even though the sports presenter said he'd be speaking to Robbie and the Man of the Match – Robbie's best friend Terry Dawson – I thought, *Fine. I can do this. I will sit, all dignified, while the biggest pair of a-holes this side of the equator gloat about their success on national TV.* And I made a proper good go of it too, until the presenter asked Robbie how he'd felt about starting on the bench.

"Well, obviously I wasn't happy about it."

"Stephen Campbell didn't have a good game today, did he?" continued the presenter. "Do you think the manager should have picked you to start instead?"

"Well—"

"Of course he should have picked Robbie," interrupted Terry. "But trust me, it's not the first time someone's made that mistake!"

Terry and Robbie began to laugh.

I blushed.

Gary's jaw dropped open.

And Malibu and Dad looked gutted for me.

So, I thought about it for a second: *Be big. Be strong.*

Then I jumped out of the chair and shouted, "Fuck you – dickheads!" at the TV screen and stormed out. I could hear Dad apologizing to Mrs Johnson about my "disgusting language" as I marched towards the kitchen. OK, it wasn't the best representation of the Bennet family – I know that. But when the red mist comes down, you don't have time to check yourself, do you? Anyway, after I calmed down a bit, I went back and apologized, then politely announced that I didn't feel well and asked Dad to take me home.

"Wait a minute, Rem," Malibu called out as we got to the front door. I turned and waited for her to waddle up to me as fast as she could. "You need *this*," she said, handing over the magazine she was carrying. "Page twenty-five. Zoe Westwick. Relationship tips." ☺

Been trying to get hold of Stephen ever since. Left two voicemail messages but he hasn't got back to me. ☹

8.30 P.M.

Still getting Stephen's voicemail.

Reflected on my behaviour at Mal's house. Decided that from now on I will be queen of self-control. Sent Mal a text.

Me: *Hey sis, sorry about earlier. How about coming in for that VJ tomorrow to make up for it? xx*

And she sent back: *Yay! Cu about 11. PS Potty-mouth incident now forgotten. xx*

Still nothing from Stephen.

"Can't help thinking he's avoiding me," I said to Kellie. Had to call someone as was going mental.

"He probably just needs to get his head together. Cos, to be honest, having Robbie outplay him like that is a bit embarrassing. Anyone else maybe – OK. But not *that* on top of the love triangle."

"Love triangle? There is no love triangle," I snapped.

"Yeah. But you know what I mean."

"No, I don't. That makes it sound like there's something going on with me and Robbie."

"But you must have some feelings for him still?"

"Nope. None."

"So why haven't you gone to watch Stephen play?"

"Er… Well… OK, I have feelings like *hate* and I'm sure he hates me too, so I know it'll be awkward to be in the players' lounge together. But that's all it is. Seriously, there's no comparison. If I had to spread them both on toast, Robbie would be Marmite and Stephen would be the best ever strawberry jam." As I'd already told Malibu, I thought I might as well tell Kellie too. "I love Stephen. Proper love. Not school crush crap."

"Oh." She didn't sound very happy for me.

"Why, what's wrong with that?"

"Nothing. It's just … well, it's only been three weeks."

"Since we got back together – yeah. But I felt it when we met in Turkey, to be honest. And then last week, when we finally—"

Whip-whoo, she wolf-whistled.

"Kel, why do you always have to cheapen things?"

"OK. Shagged then."

"That's even worse. And anyway, it was more than that. It was…" I couldn't resist smiling. "Look, I know it might sound poncey but it was special."

"Yeah, I know, I know, the moon and stars aligned," she groaned. "Does he love you too?"

"I dunno." I sighed. "Thought he might before, but tonight hasn't filled me with confidence."

"Well, there's only one way to find out. Just ask him."

"Yeah, right," I scoffed. "Hi Stephen. How are you? Do you love me? Yeah, people have conversations like that every day. This isn't *EastEnders*, Kel."

"OK, well don't ask him then. Tell him yourself. See what he says. At least then you'll know where you stand. Plus that will make him feel better about the love triangle."

"Kel!"

"I mean the fact that there definitely *isn't* one."

"He knows there isn't one," I told her.

10.30 P.M.

Mum knocked on the door earlier and asked if I was all right.

"I heard Stephen had a bad game. Don't worry, love, Newcastle are renowned for their tough defence."

Mum knows even less about football than I do, so it was obviously a line that Alan had fed her.

"All right, Mum. I'm over it already. OK–aaay?"

Blooming hate this house sometimes. #NeedPrivacy

Stephen still hasn't called. And all I get is voicemail. He's clearly turned off his phone.

Maybe he's had enough of me. Wants a PROPER girl-friend who will be glad to go to games. One who actually likes football. And hasn't made him part of a poxy non-love triangle. ☹

11.30 P.M.

Had given up waiting for Stephen to get in touch and climbed into bed, prepared for a sleepless night, when he finally called. Said his battery had died. I was so happy to hear from him that my bad mood instantly disappeared.

"Well done today, baby," I chirped.

"Well done?" he said in disbelief. "I was shite."

"No, you weren't. You were—"

"Absolute shite. Even my dad said so."

I hadn't meant to patronize him but he obviously thought I had.

"You're being too hard on yourself," I said, then borrowed a little from Mum and a little from Dad. "The Newcastle defence ... are really hard to crack."

"Yeah, well a certain person managed to do it," he grumbled. Confirming that Robbie Wilkins is the bane of my life. I knew I needed to make it clear that:

1. There isn't, will never be and has never been a love triangle.

2. There is an ocean between how I felt about Robbie and how I feel about Stephen.

The only way to do that was to man up and say that I loved him.

"Remy," he said at the exact same time as I said, "Stephen."

"It's OK. You go first," I told him.

There was a long pause.

"Look, I'm tired. I'd better go to bed and call you in the morning."

"Oh... All right."

"What were you going to say?"

"Me? Nothing much. Let's catch up tomorrow."

And after he ended the call, I whispered: I love you, I love you, I love you.

12.30 a.m.

Couldn't sleep so decided to finish the sales ledger. The salon made £450 profit this week (would have been £570 if the Tanarama had been working). It's the highest total yet. And I'd be skipping around if I wasn't as on edge about Stephen. I should have gone to the game. The guilt's killing me now. AND he probably thinks I'm a crap girlfriend. Hope he's not going to dump me. ☹

1 a.m.

Just finished reading the Zoe Westwick article in the magazine Mal gave me. It's about a book she's written called *How To Keep Him*. Apparently the women that have taken her advice have had phenomenal results. "Two hundred weddings and counting," she claims. Got a bit annoyed to begin with because of the first line of the article: "There's nothing more unattractive than a paranoid woman." *Humph!* I thought, *what's Mal trying to say?* But it got proper interesting when I read on. It lays out tactics to help show confidence in yourself. "Confidence," Zoe Westwick says, "is a big turn-on." So, instead of getting jealous when you notice that a female in a film or mag has caught your boyfriend's eye, the Westwick way is it to try talking about how pretty she is instead, to prove that you don't feel threatened.

OK. Can't criticize the way she looks but whenever I've noticed Stephen gawping at Megan Fox, I must admit, it's wound me up and I've started to say that I've heard this or that about her – anything negative really. Does that make me an "unattractive paranoid"?

The second half of the article went on about sharing as many interests with your partner as possible. And if you don't share any, pretend until you do. Zoe Westwick calls it "Fake it till you make it". Ugh! Can you imagine me pretending to like football?! Besides, it's not exactly one up for the sisterhood, is it? Thanks, Mal. But no thanks. Methinks I'll be giving it a swerve. Unless I'm absolutely desperate.

Dear God, please don't let Stephen dump me tomorrow.

Monday 23 February – 7 a.m.

Aaaaaagh! Must change alarm. The old-fashioned telephone *briing! briing!* sounded cool before, but with lack of sleep (due to boyfriend worries) now sounds like a drill in my head! ☹

7.15 a.m.

Showered.

Eyes: V. tired (like their owner).

Head: On my relationship. Hope Stephen's in a better mood today.

Right. Better get some make-up on.

7.55 a.m.

Malibu phoned just as I was getting ready.

"You're up early," I said.

"Yeah. Lately, the baby always starts kicking around seven o'clock."

"Well, maybe it can start working in the salon for its auntie then. As soon as."

"You tired?"

"Knackered."

"What about changing the time you open? I definitely wouldn't open at nine if it was *my* salon."

Malibu has loads of things that she would or wouldn't do if it was *her* salon. All of them do my head in.

"Mal," I groaned. "You know Kara's opens at nine."

"Yeah, but that's because Kara's twisted. Every other salon opens at ten."

"Agreed. But I'm not going to give an hour's head start to the competition twenty doors down the road."

"But Kara's still Kara early in the morning, whereas you – you're a moody-knickers version of yourself."

"I'm *not*."

"You are."

"Am not."

"Are."

"Not!"

"*See*. Listen to you now."

"That's because a *certain person* is keeping me on the bloody phone when I need to get to work."

"Fine. I'm just trying to help."

"Yes, but I—"

"Got it. I'd get a beautician to open up for me. Would buy an extra half an hour in bed at least, that would. Yeah, that's what I'd do *if it was my salon*."

"Yeah, well" – I paused – "that might be a good idea."

"Told ya. I'm full of them. Anyway, just reminding you about that Vajazzle today."

"How could I forget the highlight of my day?"

"Good. And did you read that Zoe Westwick article?"

"Yes–ss."

Ugh! I swear she's turning into Mum.

9.05 a.m.

Great. Nothing like bumping into your old, smarmy boss – the competition twenty doors down – when you look and feel like crap. Yet another thing Malibu's right about: whatever time of day, Kara is still Kara. She's well up herself, 24/7.

"Oh, someone did say that you open at nine like we do," she said. "How's business – busy?"

"Brilliant. Couldn't be better," I told her as I unlocked

the salon's door. "How's it going with you?"

"Oh, extraordinarily well."

"Great," I said, even though I knew she was lying. With the recession on, Kara's is way too expensive.

"Oh, um … Remy," she called. "I heard you have a problem with your Tanarama booth. Call me old-fashioned but I've always said that I'd rather invest in people over machines. Granted, it may take a little longer but you just can't beat the personal touch. Anyway, please feel free to send people along to us until it's fixed."

"Actually, it should be getting fixed today," I pretended, "so I doubt that will happen."

"OK. Well, here's hoping the salon works out for you."

Works out for me? Blooming cheek. Tah-dah! is going to be a great success – end of. Ugh! Hate the way she still makes me feel like Remy "the apprentice beautician" rather than Remy "the badass businesswoman" … who is, admittedly, slightly grumpy this morning.

I love Malibu's idea of getting one of the beauticians to open the salon for me, but it's a big responsibility – she'll have to be trustworthy and hard-working. So decided to bring my diary with me to write notes about them as they work. Good things. Bad things. And this is the genius part: will secretly award points – the first beautician to reach fifty will win!

Got a name for the competition too: Salon Idol!

CONTESTANT ONE: Lara West – 24 yrs

- Good points: A v. good beautician. Expert waxer (but bloody well knows it). Has a good set of clients.

- Bad points: Suspect that Lara thinks I don't know what I'm doing. OK, maybe I don't yet but that doesn't give HER the right to think it!

- Sob story: She used to work from home but neighbours complained about her clients parking in front of their drive. They even got a few of them clamped. That's why Lara thinks it's easier to rent a space from me.

CONTESTANT TWO: Courtney Hamilton – 20 yrs

- Good points: Has a v. nice way with customers. Great at selling products – kerching!

- Bad points: Tends to give adjectives a girly ending, like "horribubble" instead of "horrible". Very annoying.

- Sob story: Her hair. It's tragic. Mainly because of her toddler hairstyle. (I swear it's been cut by her mum and lined up with a bowl.)

• Good points: Super quick at manicures.

• Bad points: Corrects people when they call her Spanish by saying that she's Catalan. She did explain the difference to me once but my mind wandered (never been into history) so I'm still clueless as to why Barcelona (where she comes from) isn't really Spain. Also, don't know if it's because things are lost in translation but she can be a bit abrupt

• Sob story: She's a single mum with a two-year-old son.

I usually like the beauticians to arrive ten minutes before opening time. It's sort of an understanding, rather than a rule. But at ten to nine Isabel was the only beautician here. (Not the start I anticipated for Salon Idol.) ☹

Was going to award her a point but realized it would be difficult for her to open the salon on top of her baby duties. So decided to count her out of it.

Courtney eventually turned up at nine. "Sorry, but the trains were impossibubble this morning."

Lara got here two minutes ago. She apologized then added, "But I think you'll have to accept that we'll be late now and then, if you're going to have a nine o'clock opening time."

"Well Isabel seemed to manage it," I told her.

Anyhow, I'm v. disappointed and have decided to award them both zero points.

OMG. Feel like a judge on Eurovision!

10.30 a.m.

The Salon Idol competition is hotting up. Lara has had two customers – both for waxing. Courtney has only had one, though it was for a couple of treatments – manicure and pedicure. So going to give them both two points.

Tried James earlier (as forgot to call him back yesterday) but only got his voicemail. Probably a good thing, as still majorly pissed off about him calling me a gold-digger.

I've just phoned Tanarama's UK head office to get them to send an engineer to fix the spray-tan booth. Have also done my first treatment of the day – an eyebrow wax for Vicky Lynch. She requested me. Vicky was a regular at Kara's but came to the salon opening party and said she was very impressed, especially with our prices.

"They're so much cheaper than Kara's."

"Yeah. Well, you're getting the promotional prices at the moment but even when they stop, we'll be cheaper."

"Perfect. As long as you're just as good of course."

"Oh, we are," I said as I escorted her up to the waxing room.

But the real proof of that will be whether she comes back.

Malibu has cancelled her vajazzle.

"Got my wires crossed," she said. "It's pregnancy yoga today. Have to try and keep my bits the same for after I've had a baby, if you know what I mean. It's all about the perineum, they make you squeeze it in and—"

I actually pulled the phone away from my ear and shouted, "Too much information."

Was relieved to get out of it, to be honest, so didn't make a fuss. "No worries. Enjoy your class."

Besides, the spare time won't be wasted because if a client doesn't walk in, I'll just spend it doing some more ~~spying~~ observing for Salon Idol.

11.30 a.m.

OMG. Can't believe Amy "local bike" Fitzgerald had the cheek to walk through the door!

Said she wanted to use the Tanarama booth because she's heard good things about it. I was going to tell her it wasn't working – honestly I was – but then she started boasting about Lance Wilson…

"Lance loves me brown. And I want to be the perfect colour to go with my wedding dress."

"What colour's the dress?"

"White."

"Oh." Does she have no shame?

"Lance helped me pick it. He's got the best taste. It's a bustier dress because he loves my boobs. Well, he says he loves my everything. We only got engaged a few months ago but we're getting married in eleven weeks. Lance just couldn't wait. I suppose you don't when you're with the right person."

Humph! Obviously stealing him from Malibu wasn't enough for Amy. She had to have a little dig at her too.

"You're so—ooo right. Malibu's in the same position. She's got a Chelsea footballer absolutely gaga for her. He's bought her a ring with a rock the size of a cannonball."

"When are they getting married?" she asked putting her ring-finger hand in her trouser pocket.

"Well, the baby pops out in about six weeks. And then they'll set the date."

"Oh, is she having a baby?"

Oops. Me and my big mouth. Best play along now. Use it to my advantage.

"Uh-huh. Well, when it comes to babies you don't really hang about *when you're with the right person.*"

"So true. I've already stopped taking the pill."

"Gr—rrreat," I said. And it was probably mean of me but my next line was: "Now let me show you to the Tanarama booth."

I did warn her not to put the setting on high but she insisted. And when she stepped out, six minutes later, if I'd given her a spiky green wig, Sainsbury's would have stacked her on the carrots aisle.

"Aaaaaaaaaagh!" she screamed.

I offered her the full works as compensation – some products, a free manicure and wax. But somehow, I don't think she'll be coming back.

Don't mess with the Bennets, biatch. ☺

1.30 P.M.

A decent day has now become perfect! Stephen called when I went out to get a sandwich – and he didn't dump me!

"Sorry about last night, Boss Lady. I was tired and disappointed with myself."

"It's OK, baby. I understand," I said.

"How's it going at the salon?"

"Never a dull moment," I told him, thinking about Amy. "Oh, and I've had an idea, for a little competition. It's called Salon Idol. I'll tell you about it later."

"OK. But I already like the title so I'm sure it'll be good."

He believes in me. This is why I love him. *sigh*

Wish I could believe in him 100% too, instead of being paranoid about him dumping me or cheating on me. But it's so hard after what Robbie did.

Anyway, he's going to pick me up from work and take me out for dinner. ☺

7 P.M.

Today I turned away a total of five people who wanted to

use the Tanarama booth. Meaning I kissed goodbye to £150 ☺. Apologized to them big time and offered £5 off if they come back on Friday.

Thankfully, my other big earner went well: three of Isabel's clients bought some products and a couple of Lara's did too. In fact, that earned Lara some bonus points for the Salon Idol competition. It now looks like this:

Lara: *4 waxes, 1 manicure, 1 manicure/pedicure = 7 points.* Plus two bonus points for convincing clients to buy products. Today's grand total: *9 points.*
Courtney: *3 waxes, 2 manicures, 1 manicure/pedicure = 7 points.* But she agreed to give Jo Robinson a manicure, even though she turned up thirty minutes late, and won't finish till seven fifteen, so I'm going to give her two bonus points – one for the manicure and one for being dedicated enough to work past seven.

This means both beauticians are tied at 9–9.

<u>11 P.M.</u>

Stephen caused a massive stir when he arrived at the salon tonight. I was at the reception desk, sort of looking out for him, when he parked outside at five minutes past seven. He was in a car he's test-driving – a BMW X6. BMW's Netherfield branch said he can use it for a month before he decides whether he wants to buy one. (Apparently they suck up to all the footballers at the club.) It's a great car but, must say, when he stepped out of it, Stephen looked even better. He was wearing dark blue jeans, a Polo Ralph Lauren black V-neck over a checked shirt, and a Ralph Lauren Puffa jacket. And he just happened to have a beautiful bunch of flowers in his hand. ☺

Courtney was at the closest nail bar to the door, manicuring Jo Robinson, and I couldn't help feeling a teensy-weensy bit smug when I heard Jo excitedly whisper, "Who's that guy?" and Courtney, just as excited, whisper back, "I don't know but I think he's coming in." Seconds later, Stephen strode into the salon and fixed his eyes on me as if Courtney and Jo were invisible.

"Hey gorgeous," he said with a huge smile on his face.

I threw my arms around his neck and gave him a peck on those luscious lips.

"*These*," he said, presenting me with the flowers as we broke away, "are for putting up with me last night."

I could see Courtney and Jo were a bit embarrassed about lusting after someone that turned out to be my boyfriend, so I decided to introduce them to show I was fine with it because (a) they didn't know he was my boyfriend at the time and (b) he is fit and they're only human.

"Babe, this is Courtney and this is Jo."

"Hi ladies," he said.

"And girls, this is my boyfriend, Stephen."

"Hi," they replied in unison. Then Courtney was head down, back to manicuring again.

I was riding high, thinking, *Who needs Zoe Westwick*

tips? when Isabel walked out of the waxing room. She may be the oldest beautician but not only is she gorgeous, she also has the best figure ever (lucky cow) – and Stephen looked at her a little longer than necessary, in my opinion.

"This is Isabel," I said, as she put on her coat.

"Hi," they both went. And I swear Stephen's smile at Isabel was way bigger than the one he'd given me. I'm seriously brewing about it. But as we've only just made up, I've decided not to say anything – YET.

Mum was proper impressed with the flowers. We dropped them off on the way to the restaurant.

"Ooh, they're nice, love. Aren't they, my hunky monkey?"

Mum and Alan were eating dinner.

"Oh yeah. Almost as gorgeous as you, Ally Wally."

Ugh! I cannot leave that house quick enough. So–ooo glad I'm staying at Stephen's tonight. Even packed a slinky little La Senza number – Isabel, schmizabel.

Dinner was amazeballs! It was at a restaurant called Docklands' Finest, right by Stephen's hotel, and because he'd booked a table by the window, the River Thames was our backdrop.

Over starters, he talked about wanting to move out of the hotel.

"The club have said they're fine to keep paying the room bill for another five months, but nothing beats having your own place," he told me. "So I called a few estate agents today. Hopefully something will turn up." He wants an apartment rather than a big house like some of the other lads. "A house is for when you've got kids to fill it with."

Ah yes, Ewan and Kirsty, I thought.

As we waited for our main course, Stephen asked me to name my top three films. *Titanic* came first (obviously), and second place was a close-run thing between *Inception* and Baz Luhrmann's *Romeo and Juliet.*

"Did anything without Leonardo DiCaprio in it stand a chance?"

"No."

"Didn't think so."

"What are yours – *Transformers 1, 2,* and *3*?"

"Naw. Megan's not in the third one."

"Oh yeah, forgot."

"It's actually *Star Wars.* All six of them."

"*Star Wars* is my…" Was going to say "worst nightmare" but then remembered the way he'd smiled at Isabel. Maybe it was time to ramp things up a bit. "…fourth favourite film," I bluffed.

OK. So, I used a Zoe Westwick tip. But I don't feel guilty about it because it worked purrfectly.

"Naw way. Is that the first film or one from the series?" he asked, chuffed to discover our "shared interest".

"Um… All of them," I told him, and then we went on to have a good chat about the merits of each film. Well, he chatted – I listened, nodded and said a v. enthusiastic "Oh yeah" in the right places.

All righty then, he's out of the bathroom; now it's all

mine. Time to turn things up another notch by changing into my La Senza number. ☺

Tuesday 24 February – 3 a.m.

Wide awake. Just had an ace dream turn into a nightmare.

It began with my very own fairy-tale wedding. The venue: A castle in Scotland. The groom: Stephen – who was looking dapper in a white shirt and red kilt. Perfecto!

My dress was ivory, strapless and skintight. Even better – it looked like I'd dropped two dress sizes, down to an eight. Yippee! Would have been the best dream ever if my stupid brain hadn't gone into hijack mode as we were standing at the altar.

There we were, ready to take our vows, and the vicar only went and asked us both to say "I love you" instead of the usual "I do". Well, of course I said it in a shot. But Stephen just stood there, as if his lips were glued together.

"Go on!" I screeched. "Just bloody well say it!"

And of course, with my kind of luck, screaming that in my dream wasn't good enough. OH NO. I had to scream it out loud. And I mean loud enough to wake him up.

"Yer all right, gorgeous?" he asked, after giving my arm a gentle shake.

"Huh? Yeah, I, er … must have been having a bad dream."

"Aw. Ne'er mind," he said, looking sorry for me. He

even kissed me on the forehead before he closed his eyes and dropped off again.

Would love to be sleeping too, but still so angry about him humiliating me at the altar like that. ☹

<u>8.35 a.m.</u>

"Hmm. That's a sign," said Kellie. I'd called her on my way to the salon because I had a theory about my dream and, yep, we were on the exact same page. "I think it means you shouldn't mention you love him yet."

"No shit, Sherlock."

"Or maybe you could say it in a jokey way instead, and see his reaction. Like with Jack, we were on the phone talking and he said something that made me laugh, and I just finished the call with, 'Laters. Love ya, you big freak.'"

"'Love ya, you big *freak*'?!" I repeated in disbelief. "Are you winding me up?"

"Nope. What can I say? We're still together – so it worked."

"For *you*."

"Well, I suppose I knew it would because it worked before on Jamal and Tony … and Lucas."

"You big, one-chat-up-line tart."

"That's me," she chirped. "Oops. Battery's dying. I'll pop in at lunchtime, OK?"

She hung up before I could tell her about the way Stephen had smiled at Isabel and my epic fight back with a little help from La Senza last night, and then a major overhaul of my work look this morning. I'd got out of bed at stupid o'clock to recreate the big and bouncy hairstyle that was so underappreciated in Shoreditch (tricky to do with hotel hairdryer). I also applied some sultry make-up and unbuttoned the top three buttons of my shirt. The shirt didn't look right due to my lack of boobage (left my padded bra and "chicken fillets" at home). Managed to solve boob crisis with v. cunning temporary fix: toilet tissue stuffed into my bra. I was all done by seven-thirty. Then I kissed his mouth to wake him up.

"Wow," Stephen gasped when he opened his eyes. "Where're *you* going?"

"Nowhere. Just work," I remarked casually.

"Looks like you're taking this Salon Factor competition seriously. Thought you were Cheryl Cole for a second!"

Normally, the flattery would have worked but I couldn't help thinking, *Bet you wouldn't leave Cheryl Cole hanging at the altar*.

Still, I did smile and say, "Thank you, baby. And it's Salon *Idol*, not Factor."

"Aw, my mistake. I'll have to take yer out tonight to make up for it now."

Woo-hoo!

8.45 a.m.

Great. Here I am, having made a mammoth effort this

morning, and my Spanish, or should I say "Catalonian", competition waltzes in with her hair tied back and wearing zero make-up, and *still* looks stunning. I'm not asking for much – I just want life to be fair!

Still, on the plus side, it's only day two of Salon Idol and both Courtney and Lara have each earned an extra point for getting in before eight-fifty. This leaves them tied at ten points. Was tempted to award Courtney a bonus, though, for complimenting my hair. Only problem is, she said it was "fabulicious". ☺

1.30 p.m.

Halfway through lunchbreak. And I'm already zonked. Need a beautician to open the salon for me asap, so have decided to reduce the winning score. Forget fifty points – the first beautician to reach thirty will be crowned Salon Idol.

Was hoping to take a little power nap in the break but, unfortunately, Malibu texted earlier about coming in for her vajazzle. When I said we were fully booked today, she texted back: *OK, then, will come during lunch.* ☺

Snuck into the kitchenette for a sneaky nap anyway, but Kellie walked in just as my eyelids were dropping.

"Ooh. What's with the hair?" she said.

"Thought I'd make a little effort," I chirped before giving my "do" a theatrical flick. "What d'you think?"

"Well, it's, er … um…"

"Thanks, Kel. Your face tells me all I need to know. You don't like it."

"I wouldn't go that far. I just don't think it's very daytime."

"Meaning?"

"Well, I think it looks supercali," said Courtney, popping her head around the white screen that divides the kitchenette from the rest of the salon. She had a couple of empty glasses in her hand and walked towards the sink saying, "Sorry, couldn't help overhearing."

"That's OK," I told her.

"Am I losing my street cred?" asked Kellie. "What's supercali?"

Courtney put the glasses in the sink and turned to deliver a tone-deaf version of Mary Poppins singing "*Supercali-fragilistic-expiali—*"

"Thanks, Courtney," I cut in, cringing.

"Pleasure-rooney," she replied and walked back into the salon area.

"How random is she?" Kellie said as soon as Courtney was gone.

"Leave her alone. She's really nice when you get to know her." Thought it was only right to defend Courtney, seeing as she'd stuck up for me.

"Well, like I was saying. *Your hair* – it's more a going-out look, isn't it? Nobody has the time to get that glammed up in the morning, unless they're a breakfast TV presenter or a stupid WAG."

My eyes fixed on hers. They said: I'm seeing a footballer, you numpty.

"But not *you* of course, Rem. I mean a WAG WAG. You know, like the ones you introduced me to at Netherfield Park. All they do is preen themselves, shop and rinse their men for money. You're nothing like them."

"Try telling that to James," I sneered.

"Huh?"

"Nothing."

"Besides," she continued, "you're far from stupid. You're running your own business – you've got to be smart to do that."

She was doing her best to dig her way out of a hole.

"Yeah, yeah, yeah." I sighed, unconvinced. Decided then and there to award Courtney a bonus point for complimenting my hair, even if she does use ridiculous adjectives that are blooming annoying. She deserves the point. End of.

So, counting treatments done this morning, the competition looks like this:

SALON IDOL

Day	Courtney Treatments/ Extra Bonus	Points	Lara Treatments/ Extra Bonus	Points
	3 waxes	3	4 waxes	4
Monday	3 manicures	3	1 manicure	1
	1 man/ped	2	1 man/ped	2
	Stay-late bonus	1	2 clients bought products	2
Daily Points		**9**		**9**
	In before 8.50 a.m.	1	In before 8.50 a.m.	1
	1 manicure	1		
Tuesday	1 man/ped	2	1 man/ped	2
	1 wax	1	2 waxes	2
	"Fabulicious" hair bonus	1		
Daily Points		**6**		**5**
Total so far		**15**		**14**

1.45 P.M.

Humph! Fifteen minutes till lunch break is over and Malibu still isn't here. Will give her a call.

1.55 P.M.

Methinks I've messed up. Big time.

When I phoned Malibu to ask where she was, she whispered, "Can't come now. *I have to meet Lance*."

I was at the reception desk, and Isabel and Courtney were near by doing manicures, so I hissed, "Lance?! Are you crazy? You're not still in love with him, are you?" as discreetly as I could.

"No chance."

"Good because you'll never believe who—"

"But someone's told the local bike that the baby's due in six weeks! She counted back, went and had it out with him, and now he's bloody demanding to know whether or not it's his."

Oops.

"I've been tucked away in Surrey, minding my own business. I come back *once* for your salon opening and look what happens – some idiot works out how far gone I must be and opens their big mouth. Bloody hate west London sometimes."

"Yeah," I found myself agreeing.

"I'll call and fill you in after I've met him, OK?"

"OK. And Mal…" Thought about it but no, there was no point in confessing that I was the idiot she was looking for. Nothing would have been gained. "Hope everything works out."

4 P.M.

Have spent the time between clients watching Isabel as she's doing a manicure. I can see why Stephen gawped at her. It's her eyes. They're big and brown like the heroines in manga cartoons.

"No. No. No. Barthelona is actualee Catalonia," she's telling her client.

She needs to get over herself, though.

Still, I've decided it's best to keep her away from Stephen for a while. So, I'll get him to pick me up from home tonight instead of the salon. Will send him a text now.

7.35 P.M.

Home a little later than I wanted to be because Lara wanted a quick chat when I was locking up.

"Remy, I've been thinking. The nail-varnish rack shouldn't be behind the reception desk like that. Every time a customer wants to choose a colour, we have to walk all the way round it."

Don't want to be a Feminazi-type boss – would prefer to be a touchy-feely one. But Lara makes it difficult.

"I like the nail varnishes behind the reception desk because it's harder for someone to steal them," I told her.

"But no one's really going to steal nail varnishes," she scoffed.

"You'd. Be. Surprised."

"OK," she sighed. "If you say so."

Would normally have stewed over it all the way home but had more important things to think about – like Malibu.

Maybe the local bike came into the salon and I slipped up about the baby for a reason. Now she can finally talk to Lance about it. That should relieve some pressure: trying to hide the truth from him as well as Gary must have been a massive strain. Yes, I've done a good thing.

Reckon that's her phoning now.

7.40 p.m.

OK, was deluding myself.

"You told Amy!" Malibu shrieked down the phone.

"I'm sorry, Mal, it was an accident," I replied, mortified.

"Well, despite your *antics*, I've made it clear that my due date is 20 April, so Lance couldn't possibly be the father."

"But it isn't though. It's the second."

"So what?"

"So, suppose he *is* the father?"

"I've decided that he isn't."

Now, I've heard people can get a bit forgetful when they're pregnant. But there's pregnancy brain-fog and then there's a land, in the clouds, full of cuckoos.

"Malibu, I'm not being funny but it's not something you can decide," I told her.

"Yes, I can. I was confused before, but now I know I want to be with Gary, and that's all that matters."

"Well, that's great but the fact is—" I stopped and took a deep breath so I could calmly break something to her that should have been obvious. "The fact is that Lance is white. And Gary is black."

"*So?*" she replied, still on her own planet.

"So, Gary will be able to tell if the baby isn't his, won't he?" I snapped.

And that's when Malibu went ballistic. Said I was jealous and trying to "sabotage her happiness".

"Don't call me EVER AGAIN," she shouted.

"Hooray," I replied, and cut the call.

Going to hold her to that too.

Ugh! My phone's ringing. Bet that's her again.

7.45 p.m.

"What d'you want *now*?" I yelled down the phone.

"Remy? You OK?"

I pulled my mobile away from my ear and checked the number on the screen. Oops. It was Stephen hearing me scream like a banshee. *died*

"Sorry, baby, I had a massive row with Malibu and she—"

"Before you say any more," he cut in, "you're on loud-speaker and my friend Angus is in the car."

"*Angus?* From Glasgow?" I asked.

"Aye. That would be me," replied one of the deepest voices I've ever heard.

Gr—rreat. His best friend has also heard me howling like a banshee. To make up for it, I switched to *CBeebies* presenter mode – all bubbly and fun, fun, fun. "Hey–yyy. Hello Angus. I'm not usually that moody – *honest*."

"Well, I was starting to wonder," he boomed.

"Just picked him up from the station," said Stephen. "Thought we'd all get something to eat, if that's OK with you, gorgeous?"

"Yeah. Gr—rreat! Can't wait to meet you, Angus." *sigh*

11 P.M.

Spoke to Angus. Met Angus. Hate Angus. Simples.

OK, maybe hate's a bit strong. I don't want him to die or anything, but could do with him jogging on back to Glasgow ASAP. Unfortunately, that's not going to happen – he's booked a room in Stephen's hotel and he's staying for a week. He's only come to watch a Kings of Leon concert, so why's he staying for a whole frickin' week?!

Reckon it'll be the longest seven days in his life and mine, as I don't think Angus is my greatest fan either. He seemed to have it in for me from the start. In the car, on the way to the restaurant (v. nice steakhouse called NY), he said hello to me, and then spent the rest of the journey talking to Stephen about people back in Glasgow who I clearly know nothing about.

Then, as soon as we were sitting at our table, he started to go on about the Newcastle game.

"OK, yer didn't play yer best, we all know that," he told Stephen, "but our Angie summed it up perfectly. She said she hasn't seen you play since the old days – you know, four or five hundred in the stands – and then ter witness yer at St James's Park, in front of fifty thousand people, it gave her goose pimples. You've come a long way, Stevie. Yer got ter put these things in ter perspective. That's what Angie said anyway."

"Yeah," I agreed just to squeeze my way into the conversation. And then something – maybe the way Angus said her name, or the way Stephen blushed, or maybe just plain old female intuition – made me ask, "Who's Angie?"

"My sister," Angus replied. "She's big on football. Used ter play too. The female Ronaldo, weren't she, Stevie?"

"Aye. Easily."

"Can you imagine if you guys had had kids?" Angus went on. "How good would those bairns have been?"

WTF?!

"*Kids?*" I repeated, hoping I'd heard wrong.

"Aye. Stevie used to go out with Angie," Angus seemed proud to say.

"Only when we were wee," Stephen explained, and I swear he was squirming.

"Aye, they were done and dusted by the time they were fifteen."

Was that supposed to make me feel better? Because it bloody well didn't.

"How come she went to the game? Thought. You. Said. His. Baby. Sister. Beth. Was. Going."

"Oh yes. She was," said Stephen. "But then Angie turned up instead."

"Thought she'd appreciate it more," added Angus.

There are some things that the Zoe Westwick article didn't prepare for. Things that are perfectly fine to kick off about. Things like an ex-girlfriend coming to watch your man play a match, for instance! And I was just about to rip into Stephen when Angus asked, "How d'yer feel about football, Remy – support a team or anything?"

"Yeah, I do *actually*. Like… Loads of them."

Angus frowned. "Loads of them?"

"Yeah. Well… *Obviously* only one from England but like loads from … all over the world. Can you guys excuse me for a second?"

And methinks, under the circumstances, Zoe Westwick would be proud of the way I faked calm all the way to the Ladies. I then locked myself inside a cubicle and had a full-on rant to myself: "Frickin' Angus! And his frickin' sister!" No insulting name was good enough for him or bloody football-playing, stick-it-up-her-bum Angie.

Came out. Looked in the mirror. Fixed my make-up and hair. Right. This called for action. I plumped for "Fake it till you make it" time. Decided I supported Man United, as I do know loads about Coleen Rooney. But they were talking Kings of Leon when I got back.

"Aw, I cannae wait to see 'em," cooed Stephen.

"Aye, when Caleb sings it's like God's talking to yer, don't yer think, Remy?"

A curve ball. But it was still on: different subject – same tactic. So, crossing my fingers under the table, I said, "Oh yeah–hh. Actual God."

"Naw way. You've never mentioned yer like Kings of Leon," Stephen gushed. "I would've got yer a ticket. I feel bad now."

"It's OK, baby, I forgive you," I said, milking it for all it was worth.

"What's yer favourite song?" asked Angus. Then the waiter came with our food.

Phew!

I'd ordered a salad (would like to shift a few pounds). Stephen, a fillet steak with veg not chips. And Angus must have asked for a whole cow, judging by the size of his portion. To be fair, he probably needed it – he's huge, a six-foot-four man-mountain.

"What did yer say yer favourite song is?" Angus continued as he carved into his slab of cow.

"Um… It's too hard to say. I love them all."

"'Fans'!" said Stephen.

"Och naw, it's gotta be 'Revelry'," Angus insisted.

As they carried on debating, I tuned them out and started to think about Malibu... *She's properly helped me out with that Zoe Westwick article, and I've repaid her by grassing her up to Amy (albeit accidentally) and then arguing with her tonight. Shouldn't have hung up on her like that. End of.*

"Are you OK?" asked Stephen.

"I'm a bit tired, to tell you the truth, baby."

"Aw, sorry. I'll get the bill and we can go back to the hotel."

"Och naw—ww but we haven't had dessert!" Angus cried like a spoilt toddler.

Stephen looked at me, clearly torn. So I let Angus win – he could finally have Stephen all to himself. Just this once.

"It's OK, you guys stay. I'll get a cab home."

"Naw way!" said Stephen, giving me hope. Then he said, "*I'll* get you one."

He ordered and paid for a cab from an app on his phone, and here I am – in my room, worried about Malibu and Stephen. ☹

11.15 P.M.

Decided to swallow my pride and send Mal a text. Simply wrote: *Love ya sis. Always have. Always will.*

Hope she gets back to me before I fall asleep.

11.45 P.M.

She still hasn't got back to me. But she has all the time in the world because I can't sleep. Been wondering whether Stephen genuinely didn't know Angie was going to watch him play.

12.15 a.m.

Four hundred and twenty-four sheep and counting...

12.55 a.m.

Couldn't drop off so watched a recorded episode of *Keeping Up with the Kardashians*. The one when Kim realizes her marriage has been a big mistake. After just seventy-two days. Heartbreaking. My situation's nothing compared with that.

Wednesday 25 February — 7.50 a.m.

Showered.

Skin: Exfoliated.

Face: Debuting new tinted moisturizer.

Bag: Packed with everything I need except phone (which is in my hand).

Phone: Has two text messages. Woo-hoo!

I know about three people who could be up at this time. Stephen's one of them and so is Malibu!!!

First text message was from Stephen. He sent it at one in the morning. *Sweet dreams xx*

OK. All is forgiven. *gooey eyes* ☺

The second one was from James and must have come through while I was in the shower: *Call me asap.*

No text from Malibu. ☹

What's the point of telling me to call him as soon as, if James isn't going to answer the bloody phone? Grrr.

OMG. Mum has just shown me the new curtains she's bought for the living room. They're turquoise, with a bright-orange squiggly pattern, *circa* 1973. Ewww!

"Aren't they great?" she said.

"Um… What does Alan think?" I asked, hoping love hadn't made him blind enough to mistake grossness of the highest order.

"Oh, he loved them," Mum replied. "Said they were *a great find*."

She looked chuffed.

I sighed. "Mum, they are a great find if we'd wanted to keep out the Plague. Because those curtains would scare anything away – people, animals and all forms of life."

"Remy!"

"I'm serious, Mum. They're awful and I will not bring any of my friends over as long as they're up."

She said I was being unreasonable.

Is she seriously going to put curtains before her own daughter's happiness?

8.40 a.m.

Now at salon, sitting at reception desk, about to down an espresso. Never been a coffee drinker, but on the way here I was thinking about my argument with Mum and realized that my "unreasonableness" might have been down to it being early in the morning – Malibu's great "Remy moody-knickers" theory. Let's face it, she's been right about everything else so far. So, instead of trotting past Ace Café, like I normally do, I decided to go in. Then I asked the girl at the till to recommend a little pep-me-up.

"This," she told me as she handed over the double-shot espresso, "has been known to wake the dead."

James called as I walked into the salon. "OMG! I think the Bear likes me!"

"The Bear?" I said, putting down the paper coffee cup.

It turns out that "the Bear" is Rupert. And James was buzzing because Rupert has invited him to an art exhibition at his workplace, Villa House, this Thursday.

"*Me* at Villa House – can't believe it! *And* he said I can bring someone. Obviously thought of you."

"Me? I'm the last person he wants to see, unless he wants me to show him some 'before and after' crystal meth pictures."

I wasn't about to let James off the hook for taking drugs on that night out in Shoreditch and then being such a git when I mentioned it.

"Come on, Rem! We'd never touch crystal meth."

"You said that about E."

"But it wasn't E, it was MD—"

"Ugh!"

"OK, OK. All right, it's not big or clever. Satisfied?"

"Not quite."

He sighed. "And I'll try not to take them again."

"Nope. I need more than *try*."

"Please, Rem. We haven't talked properly for ages, which I know is my fault. And I'm sorry about that 'gold-digger' thing I said the other day. You're so–oo not one."

"Hmm."

"I really need your advice because I'm desperate to come out to my parents now."

That was the sucker punch. Whenever James gets emotional about wanting to come out, I become his shoulder to cry on.

"What time and where?" I asked.

"Eight o'clock. Shoreditch."

Oh Lawd. ☹

Espresso downed and making brain tick faster than speed of light. ☺

All beauticians present. ☺ ☺

Salon Idol score: Courtney: 20, Lara: 19.

Now, let the games begin. ☺ ☺ ☺

1 p.m.

Lunch break. I'm on a Tube heading to Shepherd's Bush to check out a flat.

This morning, I made everyone laugh when I told them about the hideous new living room curtains.

"You'll have to move out," Courtney joked.

"Too right," I said. "And you don't even know the half of it." Didn't want to go into Mum and Alan's Born Again Teenager behaviour – far too embarrassing – so I left it at that.

Then, while I was manning the reception desk, I overheard Courtney's manicure client – Anna Martin – say that she'd broken up with her boyfriend. Apparently he'd cheated on her. Anyhoo, it turns out that she's now stuck in a flat that she can't afford to pay for on her own.

"I can last another two months max," she said, "but then I'll need someone to take it off my hands."

"Oh, that's terribubble. Absolutely terribubble," said Courtney.

Within seconds I was asking Anna where it was and how much it would cost, and now I'm on my way there. ☺

<u>2 P.M.</u>

Loads to consider on this Tube ride back to work.

So... The flat is a simple studio with light wooden floors and white-gloss (almost certainly Ikea) furniture. It may not qualify for *MTV Cribs*, and the entire thing could probably fit in Malibu's dining room – plus it's nowhere near the luxury of Robbie's place – but I like it. A lot. Now need to weigh up the plusses and minuses of having my own flat:

Pluses:
1. Will make me fully independent.
2. Will not need to deal with the BATs every day. Or those curtains!
3. Will no longer struggle to fit clothes, shoes, EVERYTHING, into my tiny box room.
4. Will be able to have Stephen stay over, as any sexy time will not be overheard by bat-eared parent.

Minuses:
1. Will have to do my own washing and cooking.
2. With the lounge doubling up as the bedroom, will have to keep it tidy all the time. (Not my strong point.)

3. Oh, the most important thing, will have to find £500 a month to pay the rent. There'll be bills on top of that too! ☹

"The deposit's already been paid, so you'd just have to take care of the monthly stuff," Anna explained, after I'd looked around.

"Oh great," I replied. And if I could fast-forward six months and see the salon working out, it would be; but I don't have a TARDIS. ☹

Anyway, I told Anna that I'd think about it, but realistically it's probably too soon to take on a commitment like that.

2.45 P.M.

Kellie thinks I should take the flat.

In my excitement, I sent her some photos with the tag – "Supa-smart businesswoman is thinking about renting a flat. Woo-hoo!" She's just rung to say, "You should do it!"

"Kel, this is the *work* number," I hissed.

"I know. But you weren't answering your mobile."

"That's because I was in the middle of a treatment."

"So I take it you've finished now."

Lara was upstairs waxing, but I didn't want to set a bad example to Isabel and Courtney. "Yes, but no one's allowed personal calls on this number unless it's an emergency." (A little rule I've nicked from Kara's.)

"Yeah, but *you* are. It's *your* salon."

Humph! She's impossible sometimes.

"I've got to bomb it to my next lesson anyway. I just wanted to tell you the flat looks amazing," she said.

Hmm.

3 P.M.

In the words of Aloe Blacc: "I need a dollar, dollar, a dollar is what I need."

4.10 P.M.

As I was manning reception, I decided to play text tennis with Stephen.

Courtney has only just remembered that he called the salon. Apparently, he couldn't get through to my mobile. She was proper apologetic about forgetting though. If the Salon Idol competition was about being nice – Courtney would win it, no probs.

Me: *Sorry was out earlier. What are we doing tonight handsome?*

Stephen: *Hello gorgeous. Movie maybe?*

Me: *Yay!* ☺

Stephen: *What do u want 2 watch?*

Me: *U choose.*

Stephen: *U sure?*

Me: *Positive. xx*

Stephen: *OK. I'll pick u up from salon. How does 7pm sound? x*

As we were texting, I overheard Isabel's client – Big Sue – waxing lyrical about the cabbage soup diet. It's worked wonders on her – she's already lost ten pounds in her first week.

"The only problem with it is that you can get a bit windy," said Sue.

Isabel said she doesn't need to diet. "I am one of deeze people who can eat anytheeng I want and not put on even a pound."

How frickin' annoying.

"Isabel," I said. "Do you fancy swapping your six-thirty bikini wax with mine at six? Then you can leave early. "

"Deese would be fantasteek. More chance to get to de childminder on time."

Yep. And it also means that she won't be here when Stephen arrives. So I texted him to say: *Yes baby. 7 will be perfect. xx*

#Winning ☺

<u>6.55 P.M.</u>

Last clients of the day have left, and after tomorrow I may not need to drink coffee ever again: I almost have a Salon Idol, which equals a lie-in for me while my winner opens up. Woo-hoo! Thought it was going to be Courtney but

Lara smashed it today with four waxes, two manicure/pedicures, and a couple of her clients bought some products. The score is: Courtney: 27, Lara: 29, and all Lara has to do to clinch the title is turn up before ten to nine tomorrow.

Now just waiting for Stephen. Proper looking forward to the cinema tonight. Intend to snog him to death. ☺

11 P.M.

It's official. The honeymoon period is over.

Came to a grinding halt about a minute after Stephen came into the salon. Everything had gone to plan until then. He walked in. I slinked up to him, didn't say a word and planted my lips on his mouth. (*The first kiss of ten thousand*, I thought at the time.) Then broke away to see his most mischievous smile yet.

"You're in a good mood," he said.

"Yep."

"And why's that then?"

"I could tell you. But I'd have to kill you afterwards. And—"

I was cut off by the sound of a car horn. Not just any car horn. Stephen's car horn.

"Ah, that will be Angus," he said.

"*Angus?*"

"Couldn't leave him on his own, could I?"

I turned my head to see Stephen's X6 parked outside.

Angus, sitting in the front passenger seat, waved. Gutted, I waved back: Adios, cinema snogathon.

"No … course not," I said. "I'll just get my bag. Then we can—"

The horn beeped again.

"Stevie boy, yer've got a call," Angus boomed loud enough for half of London to hear him.

"You go. I'll just lock up," I told him, and really took my time about it too, as needed to recover from the disappointment.

Stephen was still on the phone when I got in the car.

"Och naw, I'll never be a southern softie," he was saying.

"Not while I'm about!" Angus, who'd had the decency to move to the back seat, called out.

Stephen's accent was suddenly stronger than I'd ever heard. "Yer both know I'm Glasgee till I die."

"Aw, is that right?" said Angus before bellowing, "Yer should have heard him talking to the estate agent today, Angie – he sounded more English than the Queen."

Angie? WTF?!

At that point, seeing as Stephen had barely acknowledged my arrival, I made a very loud, deliberate "Ahem."

He took the hint. "Um … anyway, thanks for helping out me mam. And, er … yeah, thanks… OK, we're just goin' to catch a film now, so I'll get the big man ter phone yer after that." Then he ended the call, started the engine and began to drive. "Saw some great properties today, Boss Lady, didn't we, Angus?" he said, trying a little too hard.

"Aye. They were great. And the estate agent wasn't too bad either."

I didn't reply.

Stephen tried again. "So what did *you* do today, gorgeous – anything special?"

Zoe Westwick would have ignored his conversation with Angie and told him about looking at a property too – "what a great shared interest", she would have said as they discussed the coincidence. But I, Remy Bennet, was busy trying to work out what Angie had done for his mum, whether she had an ulterior motive for helping (like stealing my man!) and why Stephen was so damn nervous.

Before I could answer, Angus said, "Shame you haven't met Angie, Remy. You'd love her. And she'd love you too. Although... Have yer told Angie about Remy now, Stevie boy?"

"Well, I, er... Haven't, um, really had the opportunity."

"What about just now? What about at the Newcastle game – that she wasn't supposed to go to but did *all of a sudden*?" I said.

"Only because *you* didn't," butted in Angus.

"Angus, naw. She has ter work, I've already explained," Stephen snapped. I could tell it was a sore point, but how could I explain that I didn't go because I was scared of seeing Robbie without him taking it the wrong way? I couldn't. So I stayed quiet. Thinking, *Why hasn't Stephen told Angie about me? Does he still care about her or something?*

Got to the cinema still unhappy about the Angie

situation. Stephen wasn't happy about me not being happy. And Angus chomped his way through a large cone of mixed popcorn. ☺

"What a film, man!" Angus said as the credits began to roll at the end.

"Yeah," Stephen and I sighed.

We stayed quiet on the drive to my house too. A courtroom drama was running in my head though. The case for the prosecution went something like this: The Accused: Stephen Campbell. Alleged crime: Still liking Angie McMillan. Evidence: He used to go out with her, and now she's going to his matches, doing favours for his mum, talking to him whenever I'm not around (probably). He hasn't even told her about me! Proof that he intends to get back with her.

The case for the defence: Stephen wanted *you* to come to Newcastle, not Angie. Would he really introduce you to Angus if he was stringing along Angus's sister? And if he does end up with her, it will only be after you've pushed him straight back into her arms by not going to matches, coupled with your "unattractive, paranoid" behaviour.

Verdict: I'm a numpty.

"This is silly," I said as Stephen walked me to my front door. "I'm sorry for snapping at you earlier. I think it's because I'm exhausted. Worked my ass off today. Didn't even have a lunch break."

"Really? Why not?"

"Cos I'm the hardest-working woman in the beauty industry – simples," I replied, trying to make him laugh.

He didn't, so I leant forward and kissed him, but it felt a bit one-sided to me. "Do you want me to stay at yours?" I offered. "It'll only take a minute to pack my stuff."

"Er… Naw, it's OK. It's late and I've gotta ice my foot when I get back – knocked it in training."

"Oh."

"I'll see yer tomorrow."

"But you're going Kings of Leon tomorrow."

"Well … let's *speak* tomorrow then."

"*Fine*," I replied. Remy With Attitude again.

11.25 P.M.

Just phoned Kel and told her all about Angie. "Am I'm over-doing it? They'd broken up by the time they were fifteen."

"Yeah, but it was first love. Which can be worse because loads of people hold feelings for their first love."

"Ugh! What is it with me and men?" I moaned. "I thought he was different."

"He still might be. I suppose it depends on whether or not you can trust yourself. You know – your gut feeling. Because with me, I can tell when a guy's into someone else by looking in his eyes."

"Well, that's because you know what to look for – seeing as you're always at it yourself."

"Oi! I've been faithful to Jack for precisely sixty-five days now."

"Congratulations," I said sarkily, because this is a

record for Kel. Her flakiness with men is legendary.

"Thanks. If I can do it, everyone can."

I wanted to agree with her but I don't live in a bubble –
I read the newspapers and mags, and I've even experienced
it myself. That's why I replied, "Except maybe a Premiership footballer."

"True," she admitted.

And now I'm actually depressed. ☹

1 a.m.

Trying to picture Angie. Hoping that she's a female version
of Angus – big and butch.

1.10 a.m.

Wonder if Kellie's right, and he loved her?

Bet he did. Bet he told her that he did too. Why, oh
why hasn't he said it to me? ☹

Thursday 26 February – 6.30 a.m.

Wide awake, half an hour before I need to be, fretting.
Boyfriends – who needs 'em!

6.45 a.m.

Can't stand feeling like this. But will keep calm and carry

on, as they say. Work to do. Money to make. No time to be moping about where I stand with boyfriend. And I'm not going to phone him either. No way.

7 a.m.

OK. I cracked and phoned him.

"Hey, gorgeous. What time is it?" he said with a yawn.

"Oh, um … six forty-six. Sorry, did I wake you up?"

"Aye. But don't worry about that. Everything all right?"

"Yeah… Perfect. I was just thinking about you … so thought I'd call."

"Good thoughts, I hope."

"Er… Yeah. Very good."

"Care to elaborate?" he asked playfully.

Cool. He wanted a flirt? Well, I would be Mademoiselle Flirty.

Put on a vampish voice and said, "Well, it was quite… How can I put this? Um… Look, do you still have feelings for Angie – yes or no?"

Oops.

"Angie? Of course not. What makes yer think that?"

"Well, you haven't told her about me, and you don't seem as into me as you were before. I offered to come to yours last night and you preferred to ice your blooming foot."

"Don't be daft. Why do I need to tell an ex about my new girlfriend? And I would've much preferred to spend the night with you."

"So why didn't you then?"

"I was a little pissed off with yer yesterday, to tell yer the truth."

"But I apologized for snapping and—"

"Naw. Not about that. Something else."

"What?" I asked.

"Well, I'd prefer *you* to tell me you're looking for a flat, not one of your beauticians."

It all came out after that. Courtney assumed he knew about my flat adventure and bombarded him with questions when he phoned the salon. Did he like it? Did he think I was going to take it? And if I did, would I move in straight away or wait the two months?

"She was going a mile a minute until she realized I didn't know what she was talking about."

She left him wondering why I'd never mentioned moving out of my mum's and getting my own flat. And when I didn't tell him about it after he asked why I'd missed my lunch break, he thought I was trying to hide it.

"No–oo, of course not," I told him.

It was his turn to sound apologetic. "Think we've both been getting our wires crossed."

"Sure looks like it." I put on my vampish voice again. "I'll have to find a way to make it up to you."

"Tonight?" he asked.

"You're at Kings of Leon tonight."

"Aw, yeah. So I am. Tomorrow then?"

"Deal."

Okey-doke. Honeymoon period resumed. ☺

7.30 a.m.

Showered.

Heart: Cooking with gas. ☺

Mouth: Can't stop smiling.

Brain: Doing overtime!

Just remembered that I'm going out with James straight after work, so will need to find the most "Shoreditch" thing in my wardrobe.

Hmm…

7.45 a.m.

It's designer. It works. The Queen rates her enough to make her a dame. And, most importantly, it has passed the sniff test – so even though I wore it to the NY steakhouse the other night, would it be skanky to wear my leopard-print Vivienne Westwood dress again?

Tried on a few other things but the leopard print definitely works best because it has a "vintagey" style about it. Ugh! Can't believe the word "vintage" is leaving my lips. Or how nervous I am about what Rupert will think about it.

Why, oh why am I trying to impress someone that I don't even like?!

On the way to work, I decided that if Malibu was going to ignore my texts, it was time to give her a call. So, stopped at Ace Café and bought a double espresso (didn't want to sound grumpy). I was a big ball of happiness by the time I got to the salon, and was just about to call Mal when the Tanarama engineer turned up. He was swiftly followed by Lara – earning the point she needed to win Salon Idol. Yay! Lie-in for me tomorrow! Will tell her the good news at lunch. ☺

Really rate Courtney though. When the Tanarama engineer was finished with the filters, he said the best way to tell whether I was happy with them was to give the Tanarama booth a trial run. As I'm out with James tonight, I didn't want to take the chance – turning up in Shoreditch fifty shades of orange would not have been a good look. So I thought I'd ask one of the girls to do it; thought they'd understand. Wrong. They looked like they'd rather chew glass. So decided the most sensible way to select a ~~victim~~ guinea pig was Rock, Paper, Scissors.

I was quite lucky at it in primary school, but today it wasn't happening. Lara was first out, then Isabel, leaving me to fight it out with Courtney in the last round.

I was about to lose when her hand came out to wrap around my fist. I must have looked gutted because Courtney then said, "It's all right. I'll do the trial run," and saved me. Spent the full six minutes in the booth too, even though she was trying our darkest colour – Bronze Goddess. It's a big contrast to her usual (quite pale) skin, but I thought she looked great when she stepped out. Sort of like a bowl-haired version of a Kardashian sister.

"Totally tantastic," she said when she checked herself out in the mirror.

Love it when a plan comes together. ☺

1.30 P.M.

The thing about X Factor and American Idol is that (a) the contestants enter the competition themselves and (b) they actually WANT to win it. Two major points that were, unfortunately, missing in my little contest.

Another crucial point is that those competitions offer a huge prize – a million pound recording contract etc. – whereas mine was a bit of a duffer.

"Get in half an hour earlier – why would I want to do that?" Lara asked.

"Um … er…"

"Will you be offering a discount on my rent?"

"Um… No."

"A percentage of the product sales?"

"Er… No, don't think so."

"Well, I'd rather keep things as they are then, thanks." ☹

The lunch break didn't improve, as shortly after, Stephen called to say he'd managed to wrangle one more Kings of Leon ticket.

So wanted to see him, but Kings of frickin' Leon – *shit. Shit. Shit.*

Luckily, I had a valid way out: "Oh–hh no. I'm going out with James tonight."

"I'm sure he'll understand. He must know how much yer love them."

"Yeah… True. I'll, er … give him a call."

Aa–aargh! Nightmare.

1.35 P.M.

I can't blow James out. Not now. Not when he needs me.

1.45 P.M.

Still torn between boyfriend and bestie.

What to do? What to do? ☹

1.50 P.M.

Have a plan!

2 P.M.

"They'll be on stage about nine, so it means yer'll miss a big chunk of the concert," Stephen said when I told him that I'd whizz over to The O2 after first spending an hour with James.

"I know," I told him, trying to sound gutted. "But he needs my advice."

"Well, you're a very good friend," he told me.

Aaaah. He's so supportive.

James – not so much. "*You* at a Kings of Leon concert?" he laughed after I explained my plan.

"I know. Not exactly Rihanna, are they. But Stephen loves them."

"And you must love him if you're willing to put up with *that* noise."

I smiled. "Yeah. Yeah, I do."

"*What?!*"

"Got to do a wax now. Let's talk about it later."

7.15 P.M.

Right, work done. I've slipped into my leopard-print dress. Now it's Shoreditch and Kings of Leon time. The first part of the night will need patience. The second, earplugs.

Friday 27 February – 7.35 a.m.

Showered. Moisturized. Dressed: In leopard-print dress again (stayed at Stephen's).

Last night almost had a perfect ending, though it didn't start out well. Would rather stand naked on a podium in Trafalgar Square than go to Villa House again. Couldn't wait to leave the place. It's a v. expensive and beyond-poncey private members' club, where people pay fifteen hundred pounds a year to use its swanky restaurant, bar and two lounges. Every room is decorated black or white, and sometimes they've really pushed the boat out by making the odd bit of furniture black AND white. So–oo Shoreditch.

James said he's saving up to join. "It'll probably take a year but it's worth it to be comfortable."

"A booth at Nando's is comfortable but I'm not going to pay £1,500 a year so I can always use one," I replied. "And *their* chips are £2.25!" Villa House's rip-off price for a tiny plate of chips: £4.55. WTF?!

"No–oo. I mean comfortable with the people *around* you," James explained.

And from that, I take it that he wants to be surrounded by "Shoreditch types" for the rest of his life – people who pride themselves on being individuals, yet they all have angular haircuts and wear out-there clothes.

Still, it was the most confident I've heard him be about coming out to his parents. He says he's had enough of living a double life and wants to be true to himself.

"Plus, Rupert won't see anyone who's not out. He says he'd be living a lie too."

"You can't do it for Rupert though. You have to do it for you," I told him.

"I am."

"Well, do you think your parents suspect anything?"

He shrugged. "My mum's always asking when you're going to come over again."

"*Me?*"

"I made out that I was seeing you. Hope you don't mind."

He looked embarrassed. Poor thing. "Of course I don't. Maybe you shouldn't rush into it then. Spend a couple of weeks dropping a few hints first."

"But I don't want to miss my chance with Rupert."

Rupert. Rupert. Rupert. Don't know why he's so obsessed with that guy. He's a grade-one a-hole. When he turned up, he kissed us both on each cheek again – *mwah*, *mwah*. And then he apologized for giving me evils the other night.

"I'm an absolute bitch when I'm wasted, dahling."

"It's OK."

"You look fierce today though."

"Thanks."

"So much better than that gold dress and shoes. Eww," he said, "they were just so WAG dot-com." Proving he's a bitch when he's stone-cold sober too.

He then took us upstairs, and showed us the worst art ever – seen two-year-olds do better.

I left Villa House at nine and got a cab to the concert. I picked up my ticket (Stephen left it on the door), went through security, up the escalators and made my way to my seat, arriving just as the KOL had started a song called "Charmer". Spotted Stephen and Angus straight away. (Angus is hard to miss.) They were standing up, hands in the air, singing.

"Boss Lady!" Stephen shouted over the music when he saw me. "They're on fire tonight!" Then he grabbed my hand, raised it up with his, and sang along with Caleb Followill and about fifteen thousand fans. I figured that I would have to join in (like any fan would) and luckily, the song only has about seven lyrics so I managed to pick it up.

We stayed on our feet for the five songs that followed – waving our arms and singing our voices hoarse. (Well, I'd start out miming.) And I genuinely liked the last song, "Sex On Fire". Kiss FM used to play a dance version of it, so I absolutely belted it out. Midway through, Stephen started to kiss me!

"Come back to mine," he said in my ear.

"Are you sure you don't need to ice your foot?" I teased.

When we climbed into bed later, Stephen told me, "Yer know, I've only ever seen the band with Angus. It's brilliant to have a girlfriend who's into them too."

And this time when we did IT it was even more special than the first – and that's saying something. So, thank you, Zoe Westwick. You're frickin' GENIUS.

Afterwards, we snuggled and his body fit perfectly against mine. We were like a pair of Russian dolls. I just knew it was the right time.

"Thanks for tonight, baby, it was amazing," I began. "Actually, to be honest, I think watching paint dry would probably be amazing with you. And look, I know we've never spoken about our feelings or anything but … maybe we should… I mean, I don't want to push you into saying something you don't want to but ... well ... I definitely know how I feel about you. You see ... I ... Stephen?"

When I turned round to look at him, he was asleep. ☹

<u>8.40 a.m.</u>

Jumped on a Tube and got in to work bang on time.

Mum called one minute later. "So you *are* alive then," she said.

"Of course I am."

"It's common courtesy to let me know if you're not coming home, Remy. You had us worried sick."

I would have apologized and explained that my battery died – I'd had to charge it at Stephen's – but the fact that she said "us" bugged the life out of me.

"Don't know what Alan was worried about. I'm not his kid."

"Do you have to be so rude?"

"No, but I'm an *adult* who happened to go out with James, then met Stephen and stayed at his. What's the big deal?"

"A real, *responsible* adult would have called their mother to prevent her from having a sleepless night. Did you not get my messages?"

"OK." I sighed. "I'll call next time."

"Good. Now how is James, anyway? Found himself a girlfriend yet?"

"No."

"That's because he's got a crush on you. You do realize that, don't you?" ☹

2 P.M.

Considering writing to the Pope, as methinks Courtney should be made a saint.

She arrived at eight forty-five and asked for a "little chat". Got the impression she wanted it to be in private so, as Isabel had just stepped in, I asked whether she wanted to talk outside.

"Good idea," she answered, so I got my coat.

"Lara said you asked her to open the salon. Is that true?" she asked as soon as we were out the door.

"Yes," I told her, a bit miffed that Lara had gone and discussed it.

"But she turned you down."

"Unfortunately."

"And all she has to do is come in at eight-thirty and check everything's where it should be, right?"

"Yep."

"Nothing else?"

"No."

"Well *that* doesn't sound unreasonabubble."

"Why, what did she say, Courtney?"

"I'd prefer not to get involved," she replied. "I just wanted you to know that *I'll* do it for you, if you like."

When I thanked her, methinks my smile was big

enough to eclipse the sun, and I've just got back from getting keys cut for her.

I tried calling Malibu while I was out (got too busy to do it yesterday). Life would be awesome if she'd talk to me. Thing is, we would have made up if we still lived under the same roof. Guaranteed. One of us would have wanted to borrow something by now – a mascara or lipgloss or whatever – and whoever was in need would break the ice: "Sorry about the other day. Erm ... can I use your Touche Éclat, please?"

"OK–aaay." Beef squashed – just like that.

It's way easier to blank me now she doesn't have to see me every day.

Her phone rang then went to voicemail. I pressed redial straight away, in case she'd run to her phone and just missed the call, but got voicemail again.

"Er... Hi Mal, it's Remy. *Remember me?* Your little sister with the *big* mouth. Anyways, call me, text, email – you can even post a letter if you want. Cool. Right then. OK. Miss you. Bye."

Felt a bit down so decided to call Stephen (he always makes me smile) but, unfortunately, Angus answered.

"We're just in the estate agents," he explained. "Stevie's agreed the rent and is about ter sign the contract."

"Has he found somewhere?"

"Aye. And it's perfect. Shall I get him to call yer back?"

"Sure."

"Oh, and Remy – are yer coming to the game tomorrow?"

I paused. Malibu might not be talking to me but I could still hear her in my ears: *Screw Robbie. Go and support your man!* And I wanted to. But why was my heart beating so fast?

"Erm ... yeah. I think so. Why?"

"Well, just if yer not, I was thinking of giving your ticket to Jenny," he whispered.

"Who's Jenny?" I asked.

"The estate agent."

Could I martyr myself one more time? Would Stephen even buy it? Maybe. But it didn't matter because I'd made up my mind.

"Sorry about that, Angus, because I'm definitely coming," I said.

6 P.M.

I just got off the phone to Stephen, who sounded happy about me coming to the match. Well ... kind of.

"It's a seven-forty-five kick-off, gorgeous. Are yer sure yer can make it? Even Superman would find it difficult to get from yer salon to Netherfield Park in forty-five minutes."

"Oh, I can outdo Superman."

"Aye, I'm sure yer can. And feel free to bring someone with yer as well."

"Oh. Didn't think you had another ticket. Angus tried to pinch my one for the estate agent."

"I bet he did. He's been trying to work his magic. You bring whoever you want. Angus can take her another time."

Right. Guess I'm actually returning to Netherfield Park then.

Now, who shall I bring?

6.50 p.m.

Dad was my first call. Robbie or the Netherfield Park WAGs wouldn't dare have a go at me in front of him; but he can't come. Although he did solve how I'm going to make it there on time by offering to lock up for me. Then he'll be going on a date!

"Is it with the same woman you brought to the salon opening?" I asked.

"Er... No. Someone else."

"Really?" I said, surprised. "What's her name?"

"Elizabeth."

"Where did you meet her?"

"Well, I'm starting to discover that when you're single and fixing the washing machines of women who are also single, the business tends to double as a dating agency."

And to think I was worried!

Tried Kellie next but knew it was a long shot because of her Saturday job at Topshop.

"Nah. Even if I could leave work early, Saturday night is Jack time ... *unfortunately*," she said in a voice I've heard many times before.

"What's happened now, Kel?" I groaned.

"Nothing. He's just boring."

"No, Kel. I know what you're like and I don't believe you. Besides, weren't you boasting the other day about how long you guys have lasted?"

"Yeah."

"So what's changed?"

"Nothing. And that's the problem. Do you know what he wants to do tomorrow night? Go to the cinema."

"What's wrong with that?"

"We did that last week, and the week before, and the week before that. Boring."

"Kel, some girls have boyfriends who don't take them *anywhere*."

"S'pose you're right. Who will you take to the match?"

"Dunno."

"Aren't you nervous about facing Robbie any more?"

"Nope. More like *bricking it*."

"You should take Malibu. She'd cut him down with one look."

"I know." I sighed and was just about to tell her that Malibu wasn't talking to me, when Courtney walked by the reception desk. Something in my head went *Ding!* "But no worries. I think I'm about to get sorted," I said.

<u>8 P.M.</u>

Turns out Courtney loves football. She even knew that it

was an FA Cup match between Man United and Netherfield Park. I advised her not to book any treatments that will run on after six so we can make an early escape.

"It's an honour to go," she said. "It's going to bring real meaning to the word 'fabarooney'. Get it? Rooney... As in *Wayne*." ☹

My biggest hope is that Stephen scores three goals. My second biggest: that Coleen Rooney is there. ☺

I'm not going to Stephen's tonight. Have to prepare clothes for the big game tomorrow and also do a bit of Facebook stalking ... I mean, investigating of Angie McMillan. I know Stephen said there's nothing going on, but a girl can't help being curious about a boyfriend's ex... Can she?

Mum popped into my bedroom just as I was about to get my "stalk" on. She apologized about not making enough dinner for me and said it's because I'm hardly around nowadays. With her antics with Alan, what does she expect?

"It's OK, I'll just have some cornflakes," I said like a martyr.

Now for the stalking...

8.20 P.M.

Name: Angie McMillan
Age: 21
Lives: Glasgow
Relationship: It's complicated.

Yeah, right! It hurts to admit but she's pretty, blonde and bloody well thin! 😐

Back from our local AM/PM shop. Bought some cabbages and about to use them to make enough soup to last a week. Big Sue's ten-pound weight loss has inspired me... Along with Angie McMillan's Facebook page.

I will be thin, I will be thin, I will be thin!

9.45 P.M.

Tasty. Easy to make. Going to work miracles with my waistline. Cabbage soup, I salute you. 😊

10.30 P.M.

Phoned Kel, as couldn't decide what to wear to the match. At first she said I should play a little reverse psychology and face off the WAGs' designer obsession with a little Primarni outfit.

"Let 'em see that you can look good on a twenty-quid budget!" she said.

"Don't reckon they'll think that somehow."

"No? Well hit 'em with a work outfit then. One of the trouser suits."

She was talking about the ones I'd bought in the sales

at Zara. My "power" outfits, as I call them. V. useful for meetings with sales reps, as they wouldn't really respect me if I was dressed like a normal eighteen-year-old underneath my salon coat: skinny jeans or leggings, etc. But would a trouser suit be right for a football match?

I frowned. "Really?"

"Yeah. Lets 'em know you're a career woman, not a gold-digger, like them."

Hmm. It would be the most un-WAG-like outfit in the players' lounge, that's for sure.

10.35 P.M.

Hark, what's this I'm overhearing?

Creaking… BED SPRINGS.

Ugh! Buying ten lottery tickets this week. Not asking for millions. Just a big enough win to get out of this house!

10.45 P.M.

Have put headphones on and turned up the music loud enough to drown out the BATs. Rihanna's "We All Want Love" has just come on. Sing it, Rih-Rih.

Wonder if Stephen loves me? Wouldn't it be great if he did, and he told me tomorrow?! Maybe I'm getting carried away with the music but really want to text him something special.

Aha! Will look online for Kings of Leon lyrics.

11 P.M.

Found a song called "McFearless". Methinks it's a perfect title, with him being Scottish and all that. So I sent him this text: *Ur going to score tomorrow my McFearless. Cu soon. x*

And he sent back: *Thanks gorgeous. Ace KOL song. xxx*

Dear God, please let him say the "L" word tomorrow.

Saturday 28 February — Robbie Twot-Face Wilkins Day, Yikes!

7.32 a.m.

My alarm went off, shortly followed by my bum. I'm talking machine-gun trump.

Damn you, cabbage soup! ☹

8.30 a.m.

Showered. Moisturized.

Dressed: Grey "career woman" power suit. (Decided Kellie was right.)

Hair: The return of the Cheryl Cole ad. (Still have to hit them with something they can relate to.)

Bag: Packed with lunch — cabbage soup in a Tupperware bowl. (It will take more than a few farts to defeat me.) ☺

9 a.m.

OMG. Walked into the salon this morning to find a brand new Courtney at the reception desk. Her bowl haircut has disappeared. Instead, she's rocking extensions that have been styled in the exact same hairstyle as me. WTF?! Didn't know whether to mention it, as she was talking to a customer – our first Tanarama client of the day. *Kerching!*

"Morning, ladies," I said (decided it was best not to).

"Morning, Remy," Courtney sang back.

And the customer said, "Oh, is that your sister?" ☹

12 p.m.

Before Isabel left for lunch, she said, "Your hair. Eet looks nice. But I prefer eet when eet's simple."

When is she going to understand that we can't all be as naturally good-looking as her?

1.30 p.m.

Had my cabbage soup at one. Been farting ever since. The kitchenette now smells like death!!!

5 p.m.

If one more person mentions that Courtney looks like my sister, I'm actually going to scream.

5.50 P.M.

The roller-coaster that is my life!
1. My last customer of the day has left. GOOD.
2. Dad will be here in ten minutes to lock up so I can head over to Netherfield with Courtney. GOOD.
3. Lara thinks there's a dead rat in the kitchenette because it smells so bad in there. (Oops!) BAD.
4. In just over an hour I'm going to have to endure a full ninety minutes of football. With Courtney and Angus for company. BAD, CHALLENGING and DOUBLE BAD (in that order).
5. It does mean I get to see Stephen. AMAZEBALLS GOOD.
6. But also Robbie. SUCKS-A-LOT BAD.

10.30 P.M.

Today is in the Top 10 of my worst days ever.

Dad arrived to lock up, reeking of Lynx for his date night. While I was waiting for Courtney to get ready, I handed him the keys and asked if he'd be able to drop the sales ledger home for me.

"Um... Well, I... Do you really need it?" he stuttered. This is what the thought of going to his own home has reduced him to.

"I usually add up the weekly takings at the weekend," I explained. "But my bag's too small." I held up my dinky, for v. special occasions Chanel rip-off. "It's OK. I'll leave it till Monday."

"Oh no, you can't do that, love. It's the appraisal meeting on Monday."

"Right. Well, in that case… I'll ask Courtney to carry it," I said, remembering she arrived with a huge handbag today, to hold her change of clothes. Right on cue Courtney walked out of the loo. I had to pick my jaw off the floor.

While I was giving it "boss chic", Courtney was dressed for a flipping brothel! Her "skirt" was so short it breached the Trade Descriptions Act and should actually be called a crotch warmer. She wasn't even wearing tights with it.

"Don't you think you'll be cold in that?" I asked, seeing as it's been one of the coldest Februarys on record.

"No. I've got my coat," she said. Then she put on a pink Puffa jacket that stopped just above her waist. There was no way it was going to keep her warm, but I suppose she was brave enough to test the Tanarama booth, and now nothing was going to stop her parading her Bronze Goddess legs. They didn't look too bad either. In fact, if she hadn't copied my hair, I'd say Courtney smashed it today. It was the mother of all makeovers.

We left the salon around six-fifteen and got to the Netherfield Park stadium just in time for kick-off. I knew Angus would give a blow-by-blow account of the game as we were watching. And as I've pretended to be a Man United fan – while actually knowing nothing about football and caring even less – I thought I'd cleverly avoid being found out by letting Courtney sit between us. But I needn't have bothered. Once I introduced them, and Angus clocked her legs, I might as well have been in Peru!

"Courtney? What a beautiful name. Are yer a model by any chance?" he said. Then out came compliment after compliment. Blah, blah, blah. On top of that, Courtney could actually discuss every shot, foul, pass and save. She was like a football expert. Anyhoo, by half-time the two of them had most definitely become one.

I, meanwhile, was beyond bored. I really don't get the appeal of watching twenty-two grown men chasing after a round leather object. Although my heart beat faster every time Stephen touched the ball. He was the one good thing about today because he was easily the best player in the Netherfield Park team. Missed scoring by centimetres when he took a long-range shot that curled in the air and hit the crossbar.

"Oooh!" the whole stadium went. But, unfortunately, Wayne Rooney was on fire and scored twice in the second half, causing loads of Netherfield Park fans to leave in a huff about ten minutes before the end. I wished I could have gone home too, and skipped the players' lounge. *Be confident, Remy,* I told myself, because that's what Zoe Westwick would have said. I strode in, lagging way behind the new lovebirds. A group of WAGs were huddled together near the bar having a chat. Impact: seven metres due north.

The easiest thing to do was to change direction – left

or right – to avoid any awkwardness. But I clocked that Terry Dawson's girlfriend, Paris, was one of them, and she's always been lovely to me, so I thought I'd be big: forget the fact that she hasn't called, texted or BBMed, and smile at her. But she didn't smile back. She and the WAGs glared at me for a few seconds and moved to the other side of the room in a mass strop.

"Slut," Anna Hargreaves, the goalkeeper's wife, muttered as they went by, and they all giggled.

I could feel my face go red.

Now I can think of a hundred and one things I should have said back: gold-diggers, users, shallow idiots. But at the time, all I did was look helplessly across to Courtney and Angus for a bit of support. They were standing at the bar, exchanging flattering remarks. Would have had more support in a liquid bra. Ended up standing on my own in a corner of the room and going through my phone as if I had a trillion and one text messages, when really I had none. And I was so angry I could feel tears coming to my eyes. No way was I going to let the WAGs see that they made me cry. I was just about to leave the room when Robbie walked in. It was weird seeing him in the flesh again. I have to admit that he's still good-looking, and does dress well, but he's also still a complete and utter twot. He bowled past me and headed straight for a Katie Price lookalike (standing beside Paris) and gave her a full-on kiss. Straight after, he smugly looked over his shoulder to check that I'd spotted him. What an A-HOLE.

I was wondering if Katie Price on a budget was the girl Robbie had cheated on me with when a blonde girl I didn't recognize approached the group of WAGs. She spoke to them for a bit and then walked up to me.

"Hiya—aa. Are you Stephen's girlfriend?" she asked.

If she'd been sent to draw up a peace treaty, she was a v. strange choice. Hate to use Rupert's words but if there is such a thing as WAG dot-com, this girl was it. Her hair was a lion's mane of straw-coloured extensions, the front of her suede shoes had a platform so high, I thought a train was going to pull up, and if she had added one more gold chain to her neck, she would have hit the floor, face first.

Still, I was interested in what she had to say so I said, "Yes, I am."

"Yeah, thought as much. I'm Danielle, Tony Winter's girlfriend – he's just joined the club. What's your name again?"

She gave me a smug smile and then glanced back at the WAGs. She must have caught that Hargreaves hag Anna's eye, because Anna muttered something to the other WAGs and they all laughed. I felt my face burn again – how could I think they'd be interested in making peace with me? And did this Danielle really think I was stupid enough to believe she didn't know who I was?

Fine. If she wanted to be a bitch, I could be a bitch too. "My name? Megan Fox," I said.

"Oh, like the actress?"

"Yeah. Just like the actress. Can you excuse me for a minute?"

Wasn't sure what I was going to say as I headed for Anna Hargreaves, but I was pissed off enough to tell myself that it needed to hit her where it hurt.

"Hey Anna, congratulations," I said, smiling like all five members of One Direction were in front of me.

She looked confused. "For what?"

"You *are* pregnant, aren't you? How far gone then?" I stared at her stomach. "Hmm. I'd say four, five months. Give me a call and come to my salon – you can have a pregnancy massage on me."

Yeah, I think that just about did it.

As I walked away feeling much better, I saw that Stephen had come into the room – Angus already obediently by his side, Courtney in tow. Yes, it's childish but I actually considered launching into a big snog of my own to get back at Robbie. There was no time, though, because as soon as Stephen clocked that the twot-face was there, he said, "Let's go."

"I know the result sucks but you were excellent, babe. By far their best player," I told him as we got into his car.

He smiled. "Cheers."

"Aye, you were brilliant," Angus agreed. Then he had a fifteen-minute rant: "But the defence were useless! The strikers crap." In fact, everyone except Stephen seemed to be either lazy or rubbish. "What they needed today was ten of yer, Stevie."

Stephen told us his manager had singled him out for praise in the changing room after the game but went ballistic at everyone else – effing and blinding. It wasn't because he expected them to win against a huge club like Man United but because of the lack of effort.

"He'll definitely start yer next week. No worries about that," said Angus.

As a car is a v. enclosed space, it was not the ideal moment for the cabbage soup to make a silent but violent comeback. But it did.

"Aw Jesus, Stevie boy! What've yer been eatin'?!"

When we got near to his hotel, Courtney asked Stephen to drop her off at Canary Wharf Tube.

"Och naw," said Angus. "It's too late for yer to be travelling on yer own. I'll get you a cab."

"But I live the other side of London. It'll cost a fortune."

"Naw worries, you're worth it," he said. "Now, whereabouts is it?"

Courtney told him her address.

"Dou–ble–yew… ele-ven. Sev–en yew… ef." Angus repeated her postcode as if he was learning a foreign language, but I have to admit, I thought he was a gentleman for calling her a cab. He even waited with her in the lobby for it to arrive, while we went up to Stephen's room.

"Angus did say W11 7UF, didn't he?" Stephen checked, fiddling with his phone. "This taxi app's playing about. Not sure it's taken my payment." He phoned Angus. "Big Man, I think it's gone through but give Courtney my number and tell her to call me if the taxi driver wants paying when she gets home."

Looks like Angus isn't the gentleman I thought he was. ☹

Sunday 1 March – Malibu's Frickin' Birthday!

8.30 a.m.

Can't believe Mal has her birthday dinner today and I won't be there to celebrate. Actually woke up crying.

"You OK?" Stephen asked when he heard me sniffling.

I was facing away from him so I said, "Yeah, yeah, I'm fine. Probably just picked up a cold. I'll go and get a tissue," as there's nothing he can do about my big sis refusing to speak to me. I dashed to the toilet and silently cried it out. Stephen was sitting up in bed reading a text message when I came back into the room. He had a frown on his face.

"What's the matter?" I asked. "Is it bad news?"

"No. No. It's nothing. Look, I'd better go for a warm-down jog. We can have breakfast after that – OK?"

"Sure," I said, but he was acting weird and seemed to avoid making eye contact with me. But what really made me suspicious was the way he kept his phone with him when he went to the bathroom to freshen up, and then he put it in his tracksuit pocket.

"If yer need anything just call," he said as he left. "I've got my mobile with me."

Yes. I bloody well noticed!

<u>9.30 a.m.</u>

Stephen's back, taking a shower, and he's actually left his mobile on the chest of drawers. I really want to check it. Does that make me paranoid? This is the crossroads I had with Robbie: and when I read Robbie's phone messages, of course, the lying cheat was busted! Surely that experience, coupled with the way Stephen acted this morning, means it's completely reasonable to check Stephen's phone too. It's better to know if something's going on, right?

<u>9.35 a.m.</u>

Everything has been wiped. All calls *and* text messages.

Why would he delete everything? Is it because Stephen's smarter than Robbie? Smart enough to get rid of the evidence? Maybe I should have it out with him. But if there's an innocent reason for everything being deleted, I'll look terrible for going through his phone. Don't know what to do!!! My life is a hot mess at the minute. That's what I started thinking when Dad called earlier and we ended up talking about Malibu, even though he'd actually phoned to remind me about the appraisal meeting tomorrow.

"I haven't forgotten, Dad," I said.

"And is the sales ledger done?"

"Er… Not quite. But it will be."

"Good. You know what your Uncle Pete's like. What time will you be getting to Malibu's birthday dinner?"

"Oh … *that*. Don't think I'll be going."

"But you *have* to! It's her birthday."

"I don't think she wants me there, Dad."

"What's happened now?" he groaned (he's v. used to our fallings-out).

"Um… Just stupid girls' stuff." Couldn't tell him the real reason, Mal would be done with me FOR EVER.

"Shall I have a word with her for you?"

"Could you, Dad? Ple–eease." He's always been ace with getting us to make up.

"OK. I'll see what I can do."

10.30 a.m.

I still haven't mentioned the phone thing to Stephen. There's probably a valid explanation. So, decided to stop being paranoid. It's been bloody hard. Angus, Stephen and me had breakfast in the hotel restaurant, and Stephen could tell something was wrong with me, as whenever he asked whether I was OK, I gave a monosyllabic "yes", "fine" or sometimes an ice-cold "couldn't be better".

But then Malibu phoned!

"Hey Rem."

"Mal, I'm so sorry. And I know I've made a good job of looking like a crap sister, but as stupid as it sounds, I had your back – I swear."

"Aren't you forgetting something?" she said. Then she began to sing, "Happy birthday to me…"

"Oh yeah. Quarter of a century – you're getting old."

"Oi, you cheeky git. Just make sure you and Stephen are at The Savoy for my birthday dinner tonight."

"You want us at The Savoy? Tonight… Seven-thirty…" I repeated, then looked at Stephen to check he could come. He nodded. "We'll be there," I told her.

Stephen said he's happy for me that she called, and he's been brill about coming. Correction. He's brill full stop. I've been stupidly paranoid about all that deleted stuff on his mobile. He isn't Robbie.

And now I've got my sister back, I can't stop grinning. ☺

2.45 P.M.

There ARE three people in our relationship. One of them is blond, six foot four and a blooming pain in the bum. No wonder I've been para about Stephen, seeing as I don't have him to myself. When is Angus going to understand that sometimes a boyfriend and girlfriend need SPACE?

He was in our room, watching movies with us until about one-thirty and then said, "Aw naw, just remembered. Don't think I brought a suit with me. Will jeans be allowed at The Savoy?"

I frowned. *He can't actually think he's coming?* But sure enough: "I better not take the chance and go buy some trousers," he said. "What time is it tonight – seven-thirty?"

119

"Um, Angus… I don't think—"

"There are some decent shops in the shopping centre on the other side of the footbridge, if you need to buy something," Stephen cut in. So I threw him some fierce eyes. But he just ignored me, and before I knew it we were all traipsing across to Canary Wharf Shopping Centre. I went because I wanted to buy Mal a present – got her some yummy mummy moisturizers and massage oils. Angus is still there buying some linen trousers (even though I advised him not to). Will put my foot down and tell Stephen that Angus can't come – as soon as he comes off the phone to his agent.

5.45 p.m.

Just want to spend some time with my boyfriend, the LOVE OF MY LIFE, without his v. annoying best friend tagging along. Is that a crime? Cos Stephen made it feel like it was when I suggested that Angus shouldn't come tonight. Even though I was proper nice about it. "Stephen, I don't think Malibu has an extra space," I said. I also added that Malibu and Gary were probably paying for our meals and it would be a liberty to expect them to pay for someone they didn't know.

"Of course it would. Tell them I'll pay for him," he replied.

"Ugh! *Again*."

"What's that supposed to mean?" he asked.

So, I decided to deal with one of the many things that do my head in about Angus. "Don't you think it's a bit strange for a grown man not to pay his way?"

"The Savoy's going to be too expensive."

"What, like everything else? You've paid for every meal he's had, the Kings of Leon tickets, and I know you must be footing the bill for his hotel room too. You even bloody paid for Courtney's cab."

"Well, he's unemployed at the moment."

"Of course he is. Who wouldn't be if they knew they could live large by sponging off you?"

"It's not sponging. We come from one of the poorest parts of Glasgow. It makes where you live look like Disneyland. And this move to Netherfield Park has been massive for me financially, so if I can help my friend get out of there, I will. Cos that's what we do – we look after each other."

"More like *you* look after *him*."

"For now, but he intends to get a job. There's more work down here – that's why he's moving into the flat."

"What, your flat?"

"No, Father Christmas's. Of course my flat!"

Aa–aaaaaaaaaargh!!!!!!!!

Anyhoo, taking Angus along to The Savoy paled into insignificance after that, so called Mal and she said it would be fine. They've just dropped me home to get ready and gone to the local for a pint.

Not comfortable with what I'm wearing for two reasons:

1. Robbie bought it. Wish I could afford to burn everything he bought me – I hate him that much. But The Savoy's an upper-class place. And upper-class places need upper-class clothes. ASOS or Primarni just won't do, and the only designer gear I have was bought with his credit card. But trust me, when the money from the salon starts rolling in, they'll all be on a bonfire – even the leopard-print Vivienne Westwood – pronto.

2. I swear my butt has got bigger. Why else would this dress feel so blooming tight? Checked what Mum thought but she said, "You look great. *Healthy*. Unlike those size-zero girls on the telly nowadays." ☹

Would normally have got angry but feeling sorry for her tonight. She's not coming to the birthday dinner because she went to Mal's for Christmas. "Tonight," she said, "is Dad's turn."

Wonder how long Mum and Dad can keep up not being in the same room? ☹

Aha! Text message. Stephen must be outside.

11 P.M.

OMG. Malibu is on another level.

For the record, I'd like to say that if it wasn't for the situation, I'd nominate Gary for Boyfriend of the Year Award.

And rename him Platinumballs, too, because everything was done to perfection.

The location: Couldn't believe people like us were eating in a swanky place like The Savoy. It had uniformed staff to greet us at the door, glistening chandeliers, ornate decoration on the ceilings and huge flower displays. It was like a movie set for the ballroom scene of *Cinderella*.

"This is where the Queen was first seen with Prince Philip, you know," Dad told us. He'd obviously OD'd on the Wikipedia research because he started to reel off tons of stars and important people who'd been there.

"And now they can add the Bennets to that list," Malibu gushed.

"H'and the Johnsons of course," added Gary's mum.

The company: Even Angus was on form tonight – he actually made me laugh a couple of times. (Methinks he was desperate to impress Gary's sister, Rochelle.) And his brand new trousers made him look proper smart. Actually, everyone looked smart. But I think Dad surprised me the most. He was wearing a new blue suit that was cut more stylishly than anything I've EVER seen him in before.

"Where's it from?" I had to ask.

"Zara," he replied. My face must have said it all – *Dad's actually heard of Zara?!* – because he felt it necessary to add, "It was a present." This Elizabeth has definitely got my approval.

Mrs Johnson wore a long purple dress with a high neck. Rochelle wore a LBD that made her look sexy and chic. Gary was in a grey Savile Row suit and Malibu's silver dress was covered in Swarovski crystals – she looked like a precious bauble.

The speech: Actually the classiest thing of all. It would have been a triumph if it wasn't for the circumstances.

"Happy birthday, my gorgeous," Gary said to Malibu. "And to quote a very wise man, 'Why wait when you can start the rest of your life today?' Don't you agree?"

"Yes," Malibu said, with no idea where he was going.

"Good. Because this is why I've taken the liberty of… Arranging our wedding!"

Everyone gasped. Gary carried on excitedly. He told Mal that he wanted their baby to be born with her officially a Johnson. "I'm kind of old-fashioned like that."

"Praise da Lord," Mrs Johnson said, nodding with pride.

"So, I've booked appointments for you in four bridal departments, sorted the flowers and catering. All you have to do is come back here to The Savoy in three weeks – the twenty-first of March to be precise – and make me the happiest man alive."

"Yes!" everyone except us Bennet sisters squealed. Methinks we were both struggling to catch our breath.

"For the first time ever she's speechless!" Dad joked.

"Oh baby. It's the best birthday present I've ever had!" Malibu finally managed to say.

She was so convincing, I almost believed her myself!

Had just started this week's sales ledger when Malibu called.

"I want you to be chief bridesmaid," she said, cool as anything.

"Huh?"

"Will you be OK to get your own dress? I'll pay you back. The theme will be pink."

"Are you going through with it?"

"Of course I am."

"But—"

"Chill out, Rem. I've got two plans."

This is Malibu's grand strategy:

Plan A: Go through with the wedding, hoping the gene pool swings Gary's way.

Plan B: Go through with the wedding and if the gene pool doesn't swing the right way, Gary will eventually forgive her because, "His mum's a big Christian, Rem. He won't want to get divorced."

Is it me or is she cra–aaazy?!

Couldn't tell her that though. Not after what happened the last time I opened my big mouth.

"Wow! I'd love to be your chief bridesmaid," I gushed.

Monday 2 March – 8.20 a.m.

Showered. Moisturized. Dressed.

Head: Thinking about Malibu.

Heart: Thinking about Malibu.

Maybe I should've told her that I don't think Plan B will work.

Mum is proper excited about the wedding.

"Isn't it great about Mal?" she said when she popped her head round my bedroom door just now.

"Huh?"

"The wedding. She sent me a text last night. I can't wait."

"Yeah. Me neither," I replied with zero enthusiasm.

Just realized I haven't heard from James. Wonder if he came out to his parents? Will text: *Well???*

<u>11.25 a.m.</u>

James says: *No couldn't do it. I'm such a wuss.*

So I'm going to send: *xoxo*.

Missed my own eight-fifty deadline this morning. *slaps wrists*

Courtney looked like she wanted to tell me off. She's taking this new role v. seriously. Gotta love her for that. Talking about love – methinks she's mad for Angus. Just heard her describing him to her pedicure client. Although she doesn't make him sound like Angus – more like a Greek god who happens to have a Scottish accent. She can't stop going on about the football match either.

Courtney to EVERY customer: "We went to Man United against Netherfield Park on Saturday!"

Customer (in surprised tone): "Really?"

Courtney: "Yep. It was fabarooney. Get it? *Rooney*."

Cue me squirming with embarrassment.

Called Kellie on the way in, to ask what she was doing for lunch, and ended up telling her about Stephen's disappearing call and text logs.

"The fact that he deleted *everything* is definitely suspicious," she said. "In fact when I become a divorce lawyer—"

"*If* you become one. You still have A levels and six years of uni before you pull that off."

"It's a wrap – trust me," she replied. Kellie's wanted to be a lawyer since we were about ten. That's when we both got into *CSI*. Like everyone else into the show, I thought I'd specialize in forensics. Kellie decided DNA wasn't her bag but that we could be a team: I'd catch the criminal with my meticulous investigating and she'd then get them banged up for life – *CSI* London-style. I gave up on forensics as soon as I started secondary school and realized I hated Science. Kel dropped her plan to rid London of criminals a year ago, when she found out that divorce lawyers tend to make way more money than criminal lawyers.

"Anyway, like I was saying," she continued, "*when* I'm a divorce lawyer, deleting stuff on phones is exactly the type of thing I'll use to nail someone for adultery. OK, it doesn't prove guilt but it definitely hints at it, doesn't it?"

"Yeah." I sighed.

"Although Stephen could be totally innocent of course," she added. "What's your gut feeling?"

"I'm ninety per cent sure he's innocent," I replied, thinking about how he'd held my hand under the table throughout Malibu's birthday dinner. "But I reckon this Angie girl is dying to get her claws into him."

"It's who *he* wants that matters, not who wants him. Have you told him that you love him yet?"

"No. Every time I feel like it, something goes wrong. *So* annoying."

1 P.M.

Been thinking about Malibu's wedding a lot today. So, when Kel called to say she was going to be late for lunch, I asked, "Kel, if someone was about to make a big mistake, would you tell them?"

"Depends on *what* it was and *who* it was. Why, what have you done?"

"No, not me. Somebody – *not anyone you know* – is about to do something I think they might regret."

"Only in your opinion though."

"But as their … *friend*, shouldn't I let them know my opinion?"

"Depends again. Are they happy with what they're going to do?"

"Seem to be," I admitted.

"Then no, don't tell them."

"But I feel like I'm not being honest."

"Honesty's overrated."

"Kel, I'm being serious."

"So am I. It's selfish. Most people only want to tell the truth because it'll make them feel better about themselves. Then they can pat themselves on the back and talk about how honest they've been. Well, what about the other person's feelings? Can you imagine how gutted Tom Parker would've been if I'd told him that I was finishing with him because of his halitosis? It was much better to tell him I needed to spend more time studying for my GCSEs."

"No offence, Kel, but this is a bit bigger than Tom Parker's bad breath."

"Yeah, but it's the same principle. Why would you want to burst someone's bubble? Especially if it's going to burst anyway."

I wondered if that's what she did with me on the phone earlier when she said Stephen could be "totally innocent".

"Anyway, what happened with Robbie – anything?" she asked.

"Ugh! He's an idiot! He—"

"Hang on, my mum's trying to get through – tell me over lunch."

1.55 P.M.

I'd even given Saturday night a movie title – *Bitchfest at Netherfield Park* – but Kellie was in a crap mood when she arrived because she'd just found out that her parents might be made redundant, so we didn't get to talk about Robbie.

"Spent years slogging their guts out for the council and look how they get treated."

Isabel, who was doing a manicure at the nail table opposite us, said, "Eet's even worse in Spain."

Seeing as it was an insensitive thing to say to my bestie right then – and also because I still have a tiny flashback of the way Stephen looked at her, EVERY SINGLE DAY – I made a point of replying, "Don't you mean *Catalonia*?"

Don't think she gets sarcasm, though, because she said, "No, I mean Spain – *theee whole country*," as if I'd fallen out of the Stupid Tree and hit every branch.

To cheer Kel up, I told her that her parents were the smartest people I knew and so were bound to get another job. And that if she wanted to, I'd arrange for her dad to see a football match at Netherfield Park. "What team does he support?" I asked.

"You joking? He hates football."

"Oh. Well, do you want to bring Jack then?"

"Ugh! Football's boring enough without him adding to the mix."

"*Kel,*" I groaned.

"I know." She sounded disappointed in herself. "Maybe I'm not cut out for relationships."

"Come to the next home game on your own then," I said. After Saturday night, I don't want to go to another Netherfield Park match without some serious back-up.

"Didn't you hear me? Football's… How do I put this nicely? Crap."

"No one can hate it more than me," I told her. "But it's not about the football, it's about the WAG watching. That's proper entertainment. All the money in the world can't stop how ridiculous some of them look. One of the girls there on Saturday would have cracked you up – Danielle, I think she said her name was. She looked awful, didn't she, Courtney?"

Courtney frowned. "Don't think I saw her."

True. She was probably too far up Angus's butt by then.

I started to describe Danielle's hair, shoes and masses of gold chains. "She was a female version of Mr T."

I knew Kellie was her old self again when she said in his voice, "I still ain't goin' to no game, fool."

Everyone laughed.

"*Please* come with me next time, Kel?" I made puppy dog eyes. "I need your protection – they tried to eat me alive on Saturday night."

She smiled. "All right, I'll think about it."

Eek! Phone's ringing.

2 P.M.

Woo-hoo! Stephen has the keys to his flat. Said he's going to pick me up from work and give me a grand tour. ☺

4 P.M.

OMG! Totally forgot about the appraisal tonight, until Dad

phoned. Said he'd try to make it an informal meeting and push Uncle Pete for us to have it at the King's Head. "Um, Dad…" I began. "Stephen's just got keys—"

"Please don't try to get out of it. Your Uncle Pete's convinced you will."

"What? No, course not," I told him, annoyed at Uncle Pete's lack of faith.

Anyhoo, Stephen took me cancelling the grand tour very well.

Hmm. On second thoughts, maybe a little too well. He certainly didn't sound close to being gutted.

Will not get paranoid about it.

But hope he won't take advantage of me not being around by writing texts that he feels the need to delete. AGAIN.

4.05 P.M.

New plan! Phoned Stephen and asked him to meet me at the King's Head for eight.

"I want to buy you dinner – the food there's ace," I told him.

"Never had a girl buy me dinner before," he replied impressed. "You staying at mine after?"

It was a no-brainer but I pretended to weigh it up: "Hmm… OK then."

Maybe spending our first night together in his new flat will be the perfect time to tell him the "L" word. ☺

Before she left work this evening Courtney spent a good five minutes trying to get some info about Angus.

"I don't know that much, other than he grew up in a rough part of Glasgow and loves Kings of Leon," I told her. But with him moving his attentions from the estate agent to Courtney to Rochelle so quickly, I felt like adding, "And I don't think he's cut out for relationships."

But enough of all that. It's time to talk about Stephen's flat. There's only one word for it: amazeballs. Well worth rushing through the appraisal meeting. Not that they noticed, as I became the ultimate professional. Got out the ledger, zipped through the figures like the maths guru on *Countdown*, and then announced, "So that means we made a grand total of fifteen hundred pounds' profit in our first month."

I was happy.

Dad was happy.

Uncle Pete – not so happy.

He sighed. Scratched his head. Gave another sigh. And then admitted, "It's actually better than I anticipated. But can you estimate how much you expect to make next month, and then explain why you're so confident that customers won't disappear once the promotional prices end?"

Methinks my uncle is a glass-half-empty person.

Anyhoo, I think explaining that we'd still be cheaper than Kara's helped his mood, but Stephen walking in positively lifted it. Uncle Pete loves football, and he gave Stephen a smile usually seen only at Christmas.

My smile may have been just as big when I noticed Angus wasn't with him. *Woo-hoo!* I thought. But that little bit of joy lasted about five seconds.

"The Big Man's outside," Stephen explained, "talking to a girl."

"Who now? He's like a dog on heat!"

"Shh!" he hissed as Angus walked in, girl hanging off arm. If this new, wavy-haired "handbag" was in a BBC period drama, she'd play the part of Buxom Wench.

After introducing us Angus said, "Stevie, I was just telling Mandy about our pool. Well, I shouldn't really say *our*."

Were we making progress? Had Angus actually clicked that if there was a pool, it most definitely only belonged to STEPHEN? Answer: No chance.

"Cos we do have ter share it with the other seven apartments," he said. He went on to describe "their" apartment as if it were the eighth wonder of the world. And he had plans for a big party too. "We'll invite loads of—" He stopped just in time, thought about it and said, "nice people. Aw, and did I tell yer about our kitchen – it's fit for a professional chef. I'll be cooking yer some top meals in that, Mandy, if yer play your cards right. And what about the speakers in the ceiling – music in every room. It's the only way ter live! And Remy, just wait to yer see the TV in Stevie's bedroom – yer press the remote control and it glides out of a cupboard. How James Bond is that? And…"

Thought he was exaggerating, to be honest, but he wasn't: Stephen's flat is si–iick!

"Do you like it?" he asked, after giving me a quick tour. We were in the bedroom and he'd just demonstrated his James Bond-style TV.

"Of course. Perfect for parties. Bet you can't wait to invite loads of *nice people*."

He groaned. "Look, that was just Angus being Angus. Yer gotta take what he says with a pinch of salt."

Just then, the Big Man called out from the lounge. "Stevie, I'm about to start the Mayweather versus Hatton fight. Yer coming?"

"Boxing," Stephen explained.

I frowned.

"Are you OK?" he asked.

I know I was supposed to pretend that I love boxing too – notch up one more shared interest – but I just couldn't. Instead I mumbled, "No, not really. I've got a rotten headache," and went to bed. When it comes to boxing, Zoe Westwick and her "I love what you love" crap can go take a running jump. #ImOnStrike

Tuesday 3 March – 9.30 a.m.

It's a long Tube ride to the salon from Stephen's apartment. Twenty-two stops. And I finished reading the *Metro* after three of them. It was crap today – just pics of the *TOWIE* lot and toffs I don't know, "Out and About". So spent the rest of the time plotting a way to get rid of Angus McMillan that wouldn't result in me being sentenced for life. Hmm... 😈

But then I spoke to Malibu on my walk to the salon. How can I be losing it about Angus and his liberty-taking when she's dealing with her massive problem so well?

"Hiya, just to let you know Gary's mum has sent out the wedding invites, so look out for yours," she told me. "I'm off to some bridal dress bookings now. I've got loads but I'd love you to be there for my last one."

"Where is it?"

"Selfridges. Six-thirty."

"Work finishes at seven though."

"Surely you can make an exception this once – your big sis is getting married! Can you believe I'm actually going to walk up that aisle?" she said excitedly.

Well, no, I bloody well couldn't. But hey, who was I to burst her bubble? "I kno–oow. It's ama–aazing. See you there."

Will get Courtney to lock up.

1.30 P.M.

Lunch break. Now should I give cabbage soup one last try? Hmm.

Stephen called to see if I'm all right. "Yer sure it was just a headache last night – nothing else?"

Had he caught on at last that Angus is the most irritating man on earth? Just to be safe, I checked: "Nothing else like what?"

Good thing I did because Stephen wasn't talking about Angus after all.

"Well, yer told me about your headache once I said we were watching boxing. Probably shouldn't have. Should have put on something yer enjoy – like *Keeping Up with the Kardashians*. Would that have cheered you up?"

If Malibu can be happy, despite being up to her neck in it, I can put up with Angus McMillan. So I channelled Zoe Westwick and answered, "*Keeping Up with the Kardashians* – pah! Can't stand them. No–oo, I love boxing. One of my favourite things – *ever*."

OK. Probably overcooked it.

"Naw way. Remy, you're too perfect. How will yer surprise me next?"

"Don't worry. Still holding back the old walking-on-water trick," I quipped.

"And funny too," he chuckled.

On the other hand – he now thinks the sun shines out of my bum. Yes!

Malibu is a human roller-coaster. She was proper calm this morning, but tonight she was an emotional wreck. She tried on three bridal dresses, and every time I told her she looked beautiful, she sobbed like a baby. Wailed so loud the third time that the sales assistant came knocking on the changing-room door.

"Are you ladies all right in there?"

"Yes, yes fine," I called out.

"Is it OK to come in?"

Malibu took a deep breath and then nodded.

"Don't worry, dear," she said when I called her back in. "Weddings are stressful and being pregnant must make it worse." As she spoke, I noticed that she kept flitting her eyes from Malibu to the dress, probably making sure that the river of mascara running down Malibu's cheeks hadn't stained the cream chiffon (which happened to be my fave). "It does look beautiful on you though. Would you like me to reserve it?"

Mal nodded.

"Fantastic."

She explained that it could stay on hold until Friday and then Malibu would have to make a decision. Then she asked whether the baby was a boy or a girl – and that made Mal smile.

"Haven't got a clue."

"Oh, going for the surprise. Let me see." She scanned

Malibu's bump. "Oh, you're carrying high – it'll be a boy."

"No way. I need a little niece to help run my empire," I said.

"I don't care either way," Malibu told us. "There's only *one* important thing about this baby."

"Its health," said the sales assistant.

So Malibu replied, "Make that two then."

We helped her get out of the dress and then the lady handed over a Selfridges business card with her name and the store number on it.

"Please let me know either way by Friday," she said.

10 P.M.

Dozed off. Luckily, Stephen's ringtone – a special Kings of Leon one – was loud enough to shake me out of unconsciousness. The good thing about talking to him on the phone rather than face-to-face is that I can Google the things "we" are supposed to love as we're talking. So when he said he was in the middle of watching a DVD of Rumble in the Jungle I went, "Huh?"

"You know. The Rumble in the Jungle fight."

"Oh yeah… Muhammad Ali beat … George Foreman. With the … rope-a-dope technique."

I could tell he was grinning with pride when he said, "That's my girl."

"That is so–o wrong," said James. (Finally got hold of him.)

"Yeah but so–o right at the same time. Come on, if you knew you could pretend something and it would make Rupert be all over you, wouldn't you do it?"

"Absolutely."

"SEE. Everyone needs Zoe Westwick in their lives."

James laughed.

"How's it going with Rupert, anyway?"

"Oh, I'm slowly, but surely, grinding him down."

"Well, if he doesn't want to go out with you – he's an idiot," I said. "And what have you done about your parents?"

"Zilch. Been having panic attacks about them disowning me."

"Of course they won't. They'll probably be gutted for a couple of days – then they'll get over it."

"I hope."

"They will, trust me. But don't do it till you're ready."

I said we should meet up Friday night – me, him and Kellie – like the old days.

And James said, "Can I bring Rupert too?"

I rolled my eyes. "Sure, bring Rupert."

Now going to down a cup of cabbage soup, then bed.

Wednesday 4 March – 8.15 a.m.

Hand: Holding Malibu and Gary's wedding invitation:

Cream card, gold writing. V. classy:

Mr Gary Johnson
and
Miss Malibu Bennet

invite you to join them
at their wedding at The Savoy Hotel
on Saturday 21 March...

Head: Totally on a dress.

I saw it when I went to meet Malibu in Selfridges, in the Miss Sixty concession downstairs. It's knee-length, denim, and perfect for parties or date nights. And, seeing as I weighed myself this morning and discovered I've already lost four pounds, I have frickin' earned it!! ☺

8.25 a.m.

OMG. Let one go in the kitchen and had to evacuate straight away. Mum walked in five minutes later and said, "Jesus H. Christ, your insides need cleaning!"

Can you imagine if I'd done that when I was on my own with Stephen? So, as much as it pains me to do this, I'm finding another diet. Cabbage soup: you're binned!

Off to work in a minute. The Tanarama booth's been smashing it this week – spring's coming and it looks like everyone wants to be brown. #Kerching

Going to shoot up to Selfridges at lunchtime to get that

denim dress. It's going to be close but I should just get back in time for my two-fifteen manicure client. Yippee!

4 P.M.

On a much-needed break between clients. Been non-stop since lunch.

I made it to Selfridges, got the dress and then bumped into Paris outside!

Didn't realize it was her at first. All I'd noticed was a woman with to-die-for legs – they were as perfect as her perfect little waist, in her perfect little designer dress. I thought her walk looked familiar – hips swinging le–eeft to ri–iight. She arrived at her car – a baby-pink Mini – and raised the boot. Then, *der-der-derrr!*, I checked the number plate: P4RIS.

Why, oh why did I have to see Paris so soon after Bitch-fest at Netherfield Park?

She began stuffing the masses of shopping bags she was carrying into the boot. I kept walking, turning my head away, hoping she wouldn't spot me. But...

"Remy," she called.

Shit. Shit. Shit. What should I do?

Keep walking. Just play deaf and keep walking.

"Remy!" She shouted it this time. And it was so loud, and so obviously directed at me, that a man nearby tapped my shoulder.

"Excuse me, I think someone's calling you," he said.

Gr–rreat.

There were two options: one was to be a mega bitch and give Paris the snub of her life; the other was to turn round with a fake surprised smile and be nice.

"Wow, Paris, hello–ooo. Fancy seeing you here."

"Hey Miss 'Beauty Mogul', congratulations," she replied, then flung the rest of the shopping bags into the Mini, closed the boot and sashayed over to me. Her spray tan, make-up, hair – everything was flawless. She was a living, breathing Barbie doll. "I remember you going on about that salon. It's good to know you pulled it off."

Was I hearing correctly? Was Paris talking to me as if Saturday didn't happen? Did she think I was an idiot or something? But rather than have it out with her, I just said, "Thanks," like a wuss.

"What did you buy?" she asked, pointing at my solo shopping bag.

"Oh, nothing much. Just a dress, from Miss Sixty."

"D'you wanna lift?"

"Nah. I'm sure I'll be—"

"Where you going?"

"Back to the salon," I told her.

"Go on, let me take you there. I'd love to see it."

She seemed genuine. And a pink Mini sure beat travelling back on the bus, so I agreed.

"I've been meaning to call you actually," Paris said in the car.

And that was as much BS that I could take.

"Come off it, Paris," I replied, "We both know that isn't true."

"Yeah, OK, you're right." She sighed. "It isn't. But only because of Terry."

Paris confessed that Terry banned her from speaking to me as soon as I dumped Robbie. And she clearly obeyed – just like that – as if he were her dad.

"No wonder they're best friends," I said. "Robbie used to tell me to stop hanging out with you all the time. Said you were trouble." I could have added, "And I took no notice," but we both already knew that.

She looked embarrassed. "They're both arseholes. And I shouldn't have listened. It wasn't even worth it – cos yesterday I found out he's been cheating on me again."

It struck me that if Terry couldn't be faithful to a girl as gorgeous as Paris, then he'd never be faithful to anyone.

"Did you dump him?" I asked.

"I thought about it this time. I really did. But I love him. Besides, they've all been at it. You have no idea what they get up to on away games."

I got a bit defensive. "Yes, I do. Stephen plays poker."

"Good luck with that because Terry most definitely does not."

"Well, maybe you *should* dump him then."

"Why would I let some cow walk in and get all the perks? With all the crap I've put up with, *I'm* the one who's earned them."

"No offence, Paris, but you look miserable about it."

"Going out with a footballer's a full-time job, Remy. Who isn't miserable in their job?"

Me, I thought. Really starting to realize how lucky I am.

"There it is, on the right," I told her as we approached the salon. She pulled into the vacant parking space one shop down, switched off the engine and stepped out.

"You stuck with the name. I'm glad you did – I really like it."

While she stood outside, admiring the neon Tah-dah! sign, every man that passed nearly broke their necks looking back at her. How can someone who has that effect on men be with a plonker like Terry? Perks or no perks, I probably would have chopped off his balls by now.

I invited her in for a look around and she was really nice about everything.

Lara's just come into the kitchenette to say my eyebrow wax has arrived. No rest for the wicked.

8.30 p.m.

At Stephen's and we three are about to have a Chinese takeaway. Yay!

Then watch a documentary on the Kings of Leon. Boo!

10.30 p.m.

Well, that's two hours of my life I'll never get back!

On the positive side, at least now I actually know things about the band. Here goes…

The Kings of Leon: Three brothers (Caleb, Nathan, Jared), one cousin (Matthew). American. Brought up in Oklahoma in the South. Dad was a preacher. They grew up dirt poor. Their music sucks. The end.

Oh yeah, there was one interesting fact. Caleb and another cousin/best friend Nacho made a pact: whoever made it first would look after the other one. Angus looked at Stephen when he heard that, and they high-fived each other.

Thursday 5 March – 1.10 p.m.

One minute into my lunch break, Lara said she wanted a quick meeting.

"A couple of my regulars have complained about the new prices," she told me.

"Have you explained that they were paying promotional rates before?"

"Yes, but they still weren't happy. Did you really think it through?"

Typical. "Of course I did."

"OK. Well, I had to ask."

Grrr.

On the up side – last night Angus asked how Courtney was doing. She looked proper chuffed when I told her this. Now thinking… If Angus is here to stay (and it bloody well seems like he is), it will be much easier for me if he has to spend time with a girlfriend. Hmm. Watch This Space!

Oh, and Kellie is up for a besties' reunion tomorrow. Yay! Will text James and let him know.

1.30 p.m.

Oh Lawd. I've just overheard Isabel tell her client, "Deeze boots you are wearing. In Barcelona we say dey are uglee not Uggs."

Really need to speak to her about social skills.

7 p.m.

Going to lock up and then I'm off to Stephen's. Will pick up a Nando's takeaway as a nice surprise. ☺

10 p.m.

When Stephen let me in I instantly smelt chicken. Walked to the kitchen in a trance (was blooming starving) to find Angus, chef's hat and apron on, cooking up a storm. Grilled chicken with boiled new potatoes and steamed broccoli with garlic, to be precise.

"What's all this?" I asked.

"Stevie boy can't keep eating that shite," he said, pointing at the Nando's bags in my hand. "He's got a big match this weekend. He needs to have proper food." ☹

Gave Stephen an extra-long kiss this morning because he's off to Sunderland later for tomorrow's game.

"Will you be playing poker tonight?" I found myself asking. (What Paris said yesterday had been playing on my mind.)

He grinned. "Is the sky blue?" he answered.

Anyhoo, solved salon price-hike crisis on the Tube ride in. Will make a Tah-dah! loyalty card (like the ones they have in coffee shops). Tick off each manicure, and once the customer has had nine, they'll get 50% off the tenth one.

I also texted Malibu to see whether or not she'd made a decision about her wedding dress.

Malibu: *Yes. Going 2 get the one in Selfridges.* ☺

Me: *Good choice. It looked so beautiful on u. xxx*

Malibu: *Thanks sis. 4 everything. xxx*

Me: *Pleasure.*

Malibu: *You OK?*

Me: *Couldn't be better.* ☺

I love my life!!

1.30 p.m.

Had quick lunch meeting to tell the girls about the loyalty cards. Courtney was first to say it was a great idea but I expected that (seeing as she thinks I can do no wrong). But

Isabel and Lara seemed to like it too. Intend to speak to a print company and get a quote for making one up.

Then I texted James to say that I didn't want to meet in Shoreditch. I knew it was a possible deal-breaker but I've had enough of that place. Anyhow, he has just sent back: *Sure. Are you OK? x*

I felt like writing: *I'm fine. Just hate Shoreditch*. But he's having a hard enough time as it is, so wrote: *Yep. Brand new xx*

I am so on a roll. ☺

7.45 P.M.

There was a v. funny atmosphere in the salon this afternoon. Whenever I came down from the waxing room, all the chat at the nail bars seemed to stop. Maybe I sounded too bossy when I told the girls about the loyalty card? Dear God, please don't let me turn into the Feminazi!

Mum and Alan have just left for the cinema.

"What're you going to watch?" I asked.

"*No One Can Hear You*," Alan replied. Judging by the trailer, *No One Can Hear You* is the scariest film on the planet.

"But Mum, you hate horrors."

"Yes, and I don't intend to watch this one. If you know what I mean," Mum replied and gave me a big wink. Ewww!

"Are you all right?" she asked, looking concerned.

"Yep, perfect," I said to cover up how grossed out I was.

Debuting my Miss Sixty denim dress tonight. Now just waiting for Kellie. We're sharing a cab to Liberation – the bar in Soho that James has picked.

Kellie just texted: *Will be 10 mins. Ru OK?*

Everyone keeps asking me that today. Will send: *I'm FINE.*

Kellie's reply: *Good. Wasn't sure how u were gonna take it.*

So I replied: *Take what??*

And that's when she mentioned the *Metro* article about the scandal at Netherfield Park.

Me: *What scandal?!*

So she called.

"Apparently," she began, "a Netherfield Park player has asked for a transfer. His wife made him do it because she found out a bunch of players were bringing girls into their hotel rooms when they have away games. Hopefully Stephen isn't one of them."

Hopefully?!

"Stephen's definitely not involved," I told her. "He plays poker."

"Oh... Good. No worries then."

<u>8.40 p.m.</u>

I Googled the story.

Headline: Netherfield Boys Play Away!

Story: Netherfield Park Rangers have been thrown into turmoil following reports that some of the players, many of them married, have been inviting girls back to their hotel rooms during away fixtures. An insider said, "It's been going on for yonks but one of the WAGs got wind of it and all hell has broken loose."

The press officer for Netherfield Park said in a statement: "We've had a few security issues at certain hotels, but the matter has been dealt with and we are now moving forward."

Unfortunately, the situation has been resolved too late for one of their players. The scandal is believed to be behind defender Tommy Roberts's transfer request yesterday. Pressure to move came from Roberts's wife. The insider said, "She told him if he didn't leave the club, she'd leave him. Unfortunately, Tommy's quite easily led but it's a disaster for the team because he's one of our best players."

Tommy Roberts? He's meant to be one of the guys

Stephen plays poker with. WTF?! I want some answers. And I want them NOW.

8.48 p.m.

Voicemail. This is not the time for Stephen to have his phone switched off. ☹

8.53 p.m.

Still can't get hold of Stephen. Absolutely stewing. Don't even feel like going out any more.

1.30 a.m.

Hom^e. S$_m$a^{sh}ed. Feel like shixbhjkl.

2 a.m.

Just Vomiteeed.

2.30 a.m.

V^{o}mited…

3.15 a.m.

V$_{om}$it$_{ed}$…

<u>3.55 a.m.</u>

Dying!

<u>Saturday 7 March – 7.31 a.m.</u>

Woke up clutching my phone like a child sleeping with their teddy. Even as near to death as I felt, I must've still wanted to hear from Stephen. Checked my phone – nothing. ☹

Still feel terrible. Never felt this hung-over before. How much did I drink?!

<u>8.15 a.m.</u>

Dressed. But feel like the walking dead. Grrr.

Mum came in to check that I'm all right. She offered to make me some toast.

"No, thanks." Reckon even the sight of toast would make me want to hurl again.

"You kids have got to watch your drinking," she said.

"Even when you're depressed?" I asked.

"*Especially* when you're depressed. Were you upset about the *Metro* article?"

I nodded.

"I knew it would hit you eventually. I said to Alan you were taking it too well."

"Oh. Is *that* why you asked if I was all right?"

"Of course it was. Have you managed to speak to him?"

"No."

She gave me a hug and told me that she was sure it was going to be fine.

Really love Mum sometimes.

Told her that I didn't want to go out after reading the *Metro* story. And what a misery guts I'd been. Even Rupert felt bad for me. He bought me a cocktail. "It's a special one. It always cheers me up," he said. But it made me feel worse. Then got so hot that the sweat was dripping off me.

"Thanks for looking out for me, Mum. And sorry for being such a cow sometimes."

8.55 a.m.

Well, I'm at work. (At least in body.) Kellie phoned on my way in. Said she was worried about me.

"You were acting really weird, Rem. Do you think someone could have put something in your drink?"

I thought about it.

"Rupert," we said together.

"That special frickin' cocktail."

I told her about them taking drugs on my night out in Shoreditch. And that James promised he'd try not to do them any more.

"Well, they definitely looked like they were on something last night," Kellie said.

I called James, ready for the rant of my life, but got

voicemail. Probably didn't have the energy to do it anyway. Then I tried Stephen again. Voicemail.

"Stephen. I've read the *Metro* article and you'd better— Uggggh!" I quickly dropped the phone and rushed to the toilet just in time for what is hopefully my last puke.

I hate Rupert. Putting drugs in my drink is plain evil.

9.30 a.m.

Well, being sick over the phone seemed to work wonders because Stephen has just called. Apparently Netherfield Park's manager – Mark Keane – made everyone in the team switch off their phones. "MK", as he's known, felt they'd be inundated with calls from journalists and that would inter- fere with preparation for the game.

"Shouldn't really have it on now, but I had to phone yer. Especially after hearing your message. Are you OK?"

"Physically? I'll get over it. Mentally? Well, that de- pends on what you have to say," I said.

"Look, I wasn't involved. I've been playing poker – that's all."

"Yes. With Tommy 'I want a transfer' Roberts."

"I know how the transfer request looks but he wasn't involved either. It's just that Becky's not having it, even though I swore on my mum's life he'd been playing poker with me."

I stayed silent.

"And I'll do the same for you if yer like," he offered.

I knew he wouldn't swear on his mum's life if he was lying.

"No. It's OK. You don't have to swear on anything," I told him. "What d'you think I am – *paranoid*?"

1.10 P.M.

Lunch break. I'm finally starting to feel normal again. The brain fog lifted at about eleven-thirty – right after Isabel came back from a coffee run and handed me a double espresso. Now feel ready to face the world. I've been thinking about the silence in the salon yesterday and the fact that people kept asking if I was OK. It must mean that everyone who read the article thought Stephen was guilty. So I've sent a text to Malibu and Mum: *Just so u know, Stephen had nothing 2 do with scandal reported in Metro. He was playing poker. Fact. Love Remy x*

Now going to have a word with the girls in the salon.

1.55 P.M.

"Oh, by the way, girls," I said. "Just so you know, there wasn't any need to keep yesterday's *Metro* article a secret. And although I'm sure you had a great time discussing it, for the record, Stephen had nothing to do with the *incident*. He was playing poker. Got that? Good."

You should've seen their faces!

Courtney came into the kitchenette a few minutes ago to apologize. Although she handed me my diary first.

"Is this yours?" she checked, holding up the record of my life.

Thought I'd put it back in my bag. "Yeah, it is. Where was it?"

"On the reception desk."

Dear God, please let it have been closed.

"We weren't being nasty when we talked about the *Metro* article," Courtney continued. "We kept it to ourselves because we didn't want to upset you, that's all."

Told her it's OK and I understand, because I'm actually embarrassed about my freak-out at lunchtime now. Methinks a combination of exhaustion, whatever was in my drink, and stressing about the article briefly turned me into the Feminazi. But that's nothing compared with the embarrassment of someone reading my diary. I wonder if Courtney did...? No, she wouldn't. Thank God she found it. Courtney Hamilton: I salute you!

4.25 P.M.

Stephen's match with Sunderland kicked off at three, just as my manicure/pedicure arrived. Luckily, I was feeling much better – I'd only had waxes up until then (and had just about coped) – because the smell of nail varnish mixed with my client's cheesy feet would have made me heave if it had been any earlier.

Checked the score when I'd finished and Netherfield Park were losing 1–0. BAD.

John Miller from ADF Printers called five minutes ago to give me a price for some loyalty cards. Said he'll email me some designs later. GOOD.

That gave me the opportunity to check the score again. And not only have Netherfield Park equalized but Stephen scored the goal! Described on BBC Sport website as a looping header. Sunderland 1, Netherfield Park 1. PERFECTO.

Twenty minutes to go.

5 p.m.

OMG. Stephen scored again – a toe punt apparently (whatever that is). The match has ended Sunderland 1, Netherfield Park 2. And Stephen was named Man of the Match. Can't wait to see him. Going to do some big congratulating tomorrow night. ☺

Will Google "toe punt".

5.40 p.m.

Stephen's amazing.

I texted: *Well done baby. U deserved it. x*
And he sent back: *Ta. U up 4 'celebrating' 2mrw?* ☺
Me: *Oh–hhh yes!!* ☺ ☺
Great minds so–oo think alike.

Got home. Crawled into the shower, brushed my teeth, sank into my PJs and then tucked myself in bed by ten to eight. That's when James finally phoned.

"James, I called you twelve hours ago. I could've been dead by now."

"That would've made two of us," he replied, "I've been on the worst comedown ever."

"Yeah, well at least you took drugs deliberately. Imagine how you'd feel if you'd drunk an innocent cocktail, only to find out it had been spiked."

"What?!"

"Yep. My drink was spiked. Probably with MDF."

"That's what you build stuff out of, Remy. You mean *MDMA*." He laughed.

"Sorry, I'm not an expert on drugs like *you* and your precious Rupert."

"Come on, Remy, that's not fair."

"I'm upset, James."

"Who wouldn't be," he agreed.

"But it's about more than it being spiked. It's about who spiked it."

"Have you found out? Who was it?" he asked.

"I think… Well, I'm ninety per cent sure it was Rupert."

"Ugh! I should've known. You're so predictable, Remy. Upset about your boyfriend? Well, bloody sort him out instead of picking on mine!"

"Everything's fine with Stephen. He had nothing to do with that *Metro* story. He was playing poker. So get over yourself and listen to the facts."

"Yeah, right. A 'listen to the facts' speech from someone who's denying a whole newspaper article about her slut of a boyfriend!"

"James! Trust me, Rupert—"

"*Rupert* bought you a cocktail out of the kindness of his heart. It may have had a couple of extra shots in it, but he would never have put drugs in it! I've had enough of you and your lecturing. When are you going to work out that you're just a WAG – no one cares what you think!"

As hurt as I was, I said calmly, "You've changed, James. It's obvious you've chosen Rupert over me – and that's fine. But I don't think I can be friends with you any more."

And that was it. The end of two years with my bestie. Now going to have a little cry. ☹

Sunday 8 March – 10.25 a.m.

Wow. I slept for thirteen hours. Didn't even know that was possible.

When I checked my phone, I had three missed calls from Malibu, two from Stephen and one from Kel. Must have slept through all of them.

Malibu had called because Mum told her about me being sick.

She was shocked when I told her that I think Rupert spiked my drink – "Although James claims that he just added some extra shots."

"Yeah, right. That wouldn't make you start sweating the way you've described. And he's still out of order even if it was just extra shots, because he should have told you – you would've limited how much you drank after that."

Which I didn't. No wonder I was so ill.

"This Rupert bloke sounds like he needs strangling. But if James can't see that, you're right to stop being friends with him," Malibu said.

I asked how the wedding plans were going and she said that apart from getting the dress, she's had nothing to do with it.

"All I know is what date and time to turn up. Gary's done the lot. He's so wonderful."

"Yeah," I agreed. And then we both sighed.

Kel called to see how I was doing too. And Stephen wanted to know if I was still up for meeting up. Said he's going for a swim then taking Angus to see some tourist attractions – the London Eye, Big Ben, Buckingham Palace and maybe even Madame Tussauds.

"Yer free to come with us, Boss Lady. But if not, I'll pick you up once we've finished. Yer up for coming back to mine?"

Just you try and stop me!!

Wow. Alan actually came into my room. He's been acting like I'd eat him alive if his foot touched my carpet before now. OK, maybe he had a point, but for some reason this morning, he was willing to take a chance.

"Hey buddy. Heard ya had the mother of all hangovers yesterday."

"Yeah, it was murder."

"Ahh. That takes me back. We used to get our Friday pay packet and convert it into alcohol. Left with nothing by midnight. Reg used to say we might as well work for the brewery." Alan went visibly red after mentioning Dad's name.

"It's OK. You used to be Dad's best friend – I've got over it," I told him. "And anyway, my drinking's nowhere near that level."

"Hope not." He was trying so hard to be nice. But I could tell he was nervous. "Me and your mum are going to the King's Head for brunch to celebrate – I've finally got myself a job."

Alan's been looking for one for nearly three months. He was head foreman at the building company he used to work for in Australia, and I think he expected to walk into the same kind of job here. Wrong.

"Congrats," I told him.

"Cheers, mate," he replied. "Anyway, we were wondering if, er ... well, if you'd like to come with us?"

This would be my first public appearance with my

godfather since he became my "stepdad". I wouldn't have been seen dead with the pair of them before but thanks to the Netherfield WAGs, I now know what it's like to be demonized just because of the person you love. Besides, I don't think you can help who you love, because even when I read the *Metro* story, I couldn't hate Stephen. In fact, if anything, the time I spent hoping and praying that he wasn't involved seemed to make my love stronger. It made me realize what I'd be losing if we broke up. Just need to man up and tell him.

"Sure, I'll go to the King's Head with you," I said

"Great," Alan replied with a big grin. As he left, just before he got out of the door I said, "Um, Alan, can I ask you a question? Do you *really* like those new living room curtains?"

"No comment," he replied.

Anyhoo, better get ready because we're leaving at twelve. But first, going to take a moment to release two imaginary white doves into the sky, as a peace symbol. ☺

11.45 a.m.

OMG. What are the chances? Dad has just called and said he'd like to meet me for lunch to discuss something. I couldn't tell him I was going out with Alan and Mum – would have felt like a traitor. So I said, "Um… Can we make it a late one, like about three or three-thirty?" So I could fit both in.

"I can't, I'm afraid. I'm meeting Elizabeth. The latest I can do is two."

Two?! That was cutting it ridiculously fine. "Might be a bit difficult, Dad."

"Oh… All right then." He sounded so disappointed, it killed me.

"Go on then. I'll meet you at two. Where?"

"I'll book the King's Head."

"Oh no! I mean … really? Shouldn't we try somewhere else?"

"Why, when we know how good the food is there?"

Arguing against that would have been unrealistic – Dad knows how much I love the King's food, so I said, "You're right. See you later."

Lawd knows how I'm going to pull this one off.

1.50 P.M.

When they are searching for a new James Bond, they won't need to look any further than me – Remy Louise Bennet. Boy was I slick today.

All through brunch I was wondering how I could make sure that Mum and Alan were gone before Dad arrived. The stress of it almost put me off my stack of pancakes – ALMOST.

Turns out the BATs are big on PDAs. When Mum wasn't stroking Alan's hair, she was doing a girly giggle she'd discovered God knows where. Forget teen, this was before puberty – most probably a throwback to her infant-school days. Who knows, but I've never heard it before. Never. Not in my eighteen years on this earth. Don't get me wrong, Alan's quite funny, especially now we've smoked a peace pipe. But it was ridiculous for Mum to "tee-hee-hee" like that. Literally all Alan had to do was breathe and she'd giggle.

So—oo embarrassing.

And I definitely couldn't chance Dad witnessing them. He would have been devastated. So when Alan wondered if we should stay on at the King's to catch Sunday football, I knew my mission: get the BATs out of the King's ASAP.

If the film critics had been watching, they'd have written: "Remy Bennet's acting was more pantomime than 007." But who cares – it worked.

"Ugh, ugh, ugggh," I went, clutching my stomach at exactly half one. "I think I'm going to be sick again."

Mum sprang to her feet and was by my side in a shot. She slapped the palm of her hand on to my forehead. "Oh no. You do feel a bit hot."

"Do I?" *Ahem* "Oh. Yeah. Yeah, I do... It's ... OK. You guys stay here. I'll try to make my way back home. I'm sure I can ..." I put on the sickest voice ever and croaked "... look after myself."

"No way. Alan, get the bill. We'll have to take her home."

Now in my bedroom, supposedly sleeping it off. They're in the living room watching a movie, and I'm waiting for a loud bit so I can tiptoe out.

Prepare for your P45, Mr Daniel Craig.

Busted. Judging by my missed calls, it looks like the BATs knew I was missing about three minutes after I'd walked out the door. So I called Mum when I was on the way back from the King's.

"Where've you been?"

"Sorry, Mum. Felt like I needed some fresh air and didn't want to disturb you. You've done enough."

"I was worried sick," she replied.

Kissed her on the cheek when I got back home.

Just hoping Arnold Becket doesn't grass me up. He's the King's landlord and he was proper surprised to see I was back and sitting at a table with Dad.

"You feeling better?" he asked.

"Um... Yeah. Think I just needed a walk," I said. Methinks my nose will need its own postcode if I lie any more.

Anyhoo, Dad's lady friend, Elizabeth, was the reason he wanted a chat. He said that even though it's early days, it's getting quite serious, and he wanted to know whether I'd be up for him arranging a dinner so I can meet her. Mum and Alan are happy; Dad deserves to be happy too. So I said, "Sure, Dad, I can't wait." And when he smiled that broad smile that I haven't seen for about six months, I instantly became Elizabeth's biggest fan.

Then we tucked into our lunch. Actually managed to wolf down a chicken roast, even though I was still stuffed with pancakes. Practically rolled my way back home.

10 P.M.

Was too late to catch Madame Tussauds as Mum came into my room carrying a pile of magazines and catalogues while I was getting ready.

"As you're feeling better, you can help me find a dress to wear to the wedding," she said. Mum says "the wedding" as if she's talking about a worldwide event. Like it's bigger than Will and Kate's, Posh and Becks', Coleen and Wayne's combined. "I've told Malibu that she should try and sell it to *OK!* magazine."

"You haven't, have you?" I groaned.

"Why not? She'll make a beautiful bride, even with the bump. And they love footballers' weddings, don't they?"

She flung the magazines onto my bed and then sat down beside them.

"Come on, Remy, you look gorgeous enough."

She patted the bed to indicate exactly where she wanted me to sit.

I sighed and put down my mascara. "OK. But I don't have much time."

It took seconds to realize that Mum is taking this v. seriously. She's earmarked five dresses and they all cost a small fortune. She says she has some savings that she's going to use. "The mother of the bride *has* to look right," she said. "And tomorrow I'm starting the cabbage soup diet."

"Mum. Whatever you do – don't touch that diet," I warned her.

"Have you got your dress yet?" she asked.

"Er… No. Been a bit busy." Note to self: Don't tell Malibu about the new denim one.

"But you're chief bridesmaid – you'd better get looking. Not long to go now."

She's right of course. Just been finding it hard to get motivated about the wedding (for obvs reasons).

I met Angus and Stephen outside Madame Tussauds. Angus actually wasn't too bad today. It's funny how you get used to people. After his tour of Madame Tussauds, he had loads to say for himself. And, *inhale*, I actually found his quips about Justin Bieber and (shock horror) Leonardo DiCaprio quite funny. When we got back to Stephen's and switched on the cinema screen masquerading as a telly, *Transformers* was on. And I groaned. Stephen's Hollywood dream girl in sixty inches of HD was the last person I wanted to see. Especially when I'd eaten enough to make me feel like an elephant. Anyhoo, we cut a deal – one that Angus suggested!

"How about we only watch it until she washes the car?" he said.

"Aye," agreed Stephen. "Then, I promise you can choose any programme you want, Boss Lady."

I told them to call me when that part was over and went to Stephen's bedroom. Was glad to, to be honest, because ADF Printers had emailed designs for Tah-dah! loyalty cards and I wanted to check them out. There were five designs, and by the time Stephen declared the lounge a Megan-free zone, I had selected two favourites: a pink card that had Tah-dah! written in purple, with nine white circles for ticks and one on the end that had 50% written across it; and a white card with a pink Tah-dah! and circles. Going to show them to the girls and see what they think. Will be a good way to make up for how horrible I was yesterday.

Really up for peace at the moment and it may even be possible with Angus. Yet again, he got on the right side of me by laying into Megan's acting as soon as I came back into the lounge.

"Hmm. I see what you mean," I said. "But she is really gorgeous though."

Properly getting the hang of this showing I'm a confident woman thing. ☺

And more good news just in: Stephen is done faffing about with his BlackBerry and has just said, "Let's have an early night" with a v. naughty grin.

Sing: *Celebrate good times, come on!*

Monday 9 March – 9.35 a.m.

The loyalty cards verdict is split right down the middle.

Once I said I prefer the pink ones, Courtney agreed with me (of course). But Lara and Isabel prefer the white ones. Especially Lara – she said they look more "classy and professional". Hmm.

<u>1.25 P.M.</u>

Stephen's playing Aston Villa at home this Wednesday, and Courtney has been dropping hints about wanting to go. She's lovely enough and all that, but don't think it's a good idea to take her for three reasons:

1. Don't want to sound ungrateful (as appreciate her support) but it's kind of impossible to have a good conversation with someone who agrees with everything you say.

2. Made Kellie promise to come with me to the next home game. (Need back-up after last time.)

3. Angus.

I tried a bit of matchmaking last night.

"Naw, Courtney's a nice girl but not my type, is she, Stevie?" said Angus.

"Naw, definitely not," Stephen agreed.

Been making out that I haven't cottoned on to her hints but starting to feel guilty. I don't want to lie and say there isn't a ticket when there is one. That's why I phoned Kel to see whether she was still up for coming.

"Yeah. Maybe."

"I need a definite answer, Kel, cos someone else wants to go."

"OK. Yes then… Probably. "

Grrrrr.

This is just embarrassing now. Before she left to go home, Courtney said, "So, does Stephen expect to play against Aston Villa on Wednesday?"

"Er… Yeah, I suppose so."

"Oh–hh, I have a feeling the game will be fabulicious."

"Uh-huh. I'm sure it will."

"My feet have only just hit the ground again after the Man United match. It was so brill… And I'd love to go on Wednesday. Oops! Sorry," she said, putting her hand over her mouth. "I've overstepped the mark, haven't I?"

Right then I would have preferred to tell a child that Santa doesn't exist than tell Courtney she couldn't come to the game.

"Of course you haven't! I'll see what I can do." ☹

Tuesday 10 March – 8.40 a.m.

Stephen received a couple of text messages late last night, just as we'd got into bed.

"Who's that?" I asked.

"Probably Angus."

"What – from his bedroom down the hall?!"

Stephen went red. "Aw yeah. Forgot he lives here for a

second. Well, in that case, it's probably my agent."

"Maybe you should check. It must be important," I said, trying to not sound suspicious.

"Naww. We're busy," he replied. Then he gave me a kiss, so I went along with it. But woke up this morning with my head split in two. The positive side says: *Stephen's a great guy, even though he hasn't said that he loves me.* But the negative side is saying: *He's hiding something. That text wasn't his agent. And if he is lying about that then you can't really believe he was playing poker on away games!*

12.30 P.M.

It's been a bad morning. Lara kept making a big deal out of getting nail varnish from the rack behind the desk.

"Harumph!" she huffed when she walked by. Then "Harumph!" again when she walked back to her station with a couple of colours in her hand.

Then the customer from hell – Katie Weeks – arrived. She'd obviously been scrubbing her skin big time because she wasn't acid-orange any more, more a dark beige. She wanted the free Tanarama session and manicure that I'd promised as compensation.

"You're fine to use the Tanarama booth, Miss Weeks," I said in a polite voice.

"Mrs," she corrected.

"Oops! Sorry. *Mrs* Weeks. But I'm afraid you're supposed to book the manicure in advance."

"You didn't say that before!" she objected.

We were busy – and the last thing I needed was a scene. So I became double, triple polite. "I'm *absolutely* certain that I did. And *unfortunately*, Mrs Weeks, I'm completely booked up for the remainder of the day. *However*, I can make an appointment for you tomorrow."

"If I wanted it tomorrow, I would have come *tomorrow*," she snapped, raising her voice loud enough to make everyone glance in our direction.

Grrr. This is one of the things I hate about the service industry. The customer is always right – even when they're clearly not. And you have to be nice to them, even if they're being bloody horrible to you.

Still, managed to keep my cool (just about). "Well, I agree, it's an unfortunate mistake but—"

"It's OK," Courtney interrupted. "I can do it in my lunch break. Will twenty minutes' time be all right?"

Katie hummed and hawed for a bit and you could tell she was enjoying making us wait, then she eventually said, "OK."

1.10 P.M.

Called Stephen when I popped out to get a sandwich because I feel crap not asking Courtney to the game when she's being so nice.

"Can you get another ticket for the Aston Villa game?" I asked.

"Who for?"

"Courtney. I feel bad about not bringing her."

"Well, don't. I'm sure she'll survive."

"Unless … Kellie can't come. I'll double-check."

"Naw. Leave it. Don't really want Courtney there, to tell you the truth. It's … a wee bit awkward for Angus."

Thought I'd break it to her as soon as I got back, but walked in and saw Katie Weeks inspecting her nails as if they were under a microscope.

"There's a little smudge there," she said, holding up the offending finger.

Courtney used nail varnish remover to wipe the nail clean. Which meant she'd have to start that nail all over again – base coat, two coats of colour, top coat.

"And *there*… And *there*," Katie added.

I know I wasn't up close but they looked perfect to me. A mere mortal might have huffed and puffed but Saint Courtney simply said, "Oh, sorry. Let me fix them."

She deserves to go to the game. She really does.

Aa–aaarghh! Actually feel evil now.

Going to phone Kel. If she can't come, I'm sure I can persuade Stephen that Courtney should – Angus needs to get over himself.

1.30 P.M.

"Are you double, triple sure you're coming tomorrow?"

"Positive," Kellie replied.

"OK... Great," I told her. But she said I sounded disappointed. "Come off it, you know that's not true. It's just—" Stopped myself but Kel knows me too well.

"Did you want to bring your new supercali fwend?" she teased.

"No, course not," I said.

7.05 p.m.

OMG. Broke the bad news to Courtney and thought she was going to rip into me for a sec because her nostrils flared. OK, they only moved a teensy weensy bit, but for her that's a proper strop.

9 p.m.

Hate having to come home just so I can sort clothes for the game tomorrow. Would it be too forward to suggest I leave some clothes at Stephen's? Probably. Maybe it's worth asking just to see his reaction.

Mum cooked a tasty pasta carbonara tonight. But didn't eat it all. Had to escape because she kept going on about Malibu's wedding. And the fact that I don't have a chief bridesmaid dress yet seemed to cause her proper distress. Thought she was going to have a fit.

Which reminds me – will see how Mal's doing.

9.15 P.M.

She's so good at acting it's hard to tell that she meant it, but Malibu said she was fine.

"The baby's kicking a lot. Almost thirty-seven weeks now. It can come any time after that."

"Yippee! Can't wait to meet my little niece or nephew," I replied, crossing my fingers. *Please let the baby be Gary's.*

12.30 a.m.

Can't sleep. Keep thinking about those messages Stephen got on Monday night. Keep asking myself: *What did his face look like when he heard the message alerts?* Then: *What did it look like when I made it clear it couldn't be Angus?* And: *How did he look when I told him to check his phone? Guilty?* Basically: *Are you the man I think you are, Stephen Campbell?* ☹

Wednesday 11 March – My second home game!!

8 a.m.

Woke up and made a decision: going to stop fretting about Stephen and ENJOY MY LIFE. And I already feel two stone lighter. #YOLO

<u>8.30 a.m.</u>

Showered. Moisturized.

Hair: Not enough time so this will have to do – a slight version of the Cheryl Cole. Actually prefer it this way, to be honest. It's less glamour puss and more simple, like me.

Clothes: The red dress that I "borrowed" from Malibu ages ago. Got a little pang of sadness in my stomach when I picked it out because it reminds me of James. He loved me wearing it. Missing him badly today. ☹

<u>8.55 a.m.</u>

I'm in. Courtney seems to be her usual self, so I suppose she's over the disappointment of not coming tonight. Still, won't mention it though. Just in case.

Oh, and I phoned ADF Printers and ordered a hundred loyalty cards.

"Which ones – pink or white?" the man on the phone asked.

"Um… The white ones, please." (Pains me to admit it, but Lara's right, they do look more professional.)

<u>12.15 p.m.</u>

OMG. The Tanarama's buzzing today. As one steps out, another steps in.

Kellie arrived all dolled up for the big match.

"Can we have a quick chat in the kitchen?" she asked.

"Sure," I told her.

Thought she was going to tell me something about her and Jack. Instead she said, "Just saw your mum in the newsagent's. You didn't tell me Mal was getting married."

"Oh, didn't I? Must have slipped my mind. *Anyway*, you look good."

"Why are you changing the subject?" she asked.

"Me? Am I?"

"You know you are. Look, your mum's a bit worried. She thinks you're jealous about Malibu's wedding."

"Yeah right," I scoffed.

"Well, are you?"

"Of course not."

Aargh! My life!!!

Anyhoo, somehow Kel managed to leave her iPhone at home – and no way can she live without her iPhone, so she's just rushed off to get it. We'll be able to leave straight away once she's back because Dad has just arrived to get the keys. He's locking up for me again tonight. #BestDadEver

11.25 P.M.

Dear God, can you please, please, please erase the last five hours? Well, OK, not everything. Keep the bit where

Stephen scores and Netherfield Park wins. But I'd like to change everything else. Or, to be more specific, what I didn't need was to go into the players' lounge to discover that Danielle (owner of lion's-mane hairstyle) had taken me seriously at the last home game and actually believed that my name was Megan Fox. WTF?!

"Hi Megan. Your man played well," she said.

"Megan? Who's Megan?" I asked, frowning.

"You're Megan Fox, right?"

"Er… Danielle, Megan Fox isn't *actually* my name."

Kel didn't even attempt to hold in her laugh. At least I did. OK, I wasn't successful, but I tried.

"What did I tell you – they're as thick as shit," Kel said before I could stop her. Danielle walked away like a wounded puppy.

"Kel, you shouldn't have said that."

"Why not? It's true."

Maybe it was – but I still felt crappy about it. Especially when I noticed Danielle come back into the room a while later and stand on her own. The WAGs were all laughing and gossiping by the bar. They didn't speak to either of us. Had I got things completely twisted and she hadn't been fully accepted by the other WAGs? A few minutes later, when Kel went to the loo and Stephen was still at the bar, I thought it was the perfect time to introduce myself properly and apologize. I walked up to her and held out my hand. "Sorry about that, Danielle. It's just that I—"

"Piss off!" she shouted.

"Don't be like that. It was just a—"

"I *said* – piss off!"

Everyone in the lounge was staring at me as I made my way back towards the bar. Especially Stephen.

"I don't know what got into her…" I began. But he wasn't having it.

"I do," he hissed. "Maybe you think it's OK to mock her in the players' lounge, just like you did in your salon."

"No… I…"

"Get yer coat. Cos I'm going!" he snapped.

"But Kel's still in the Ladies."

"Tough. Meet me at the car."

He stormed out. Angus, hot on his heels, shook his head at me and went, "Tsk, tsk." I've gone right off him. AGAIN.

In a way, Danielle should thank me because a huddle of big-haired, designer-clad women formed a circle around her, no doubt offering their support against the big bad bitch. Wasn't about to stay in that room, dying of shame, so went to find Kel in the toilets. That's how I spotted her in the corridor, exchanging numbers with Netherfield Park midfielder David Joseph. ☹

Back at Stephen's now. And even though we argued about Danielle all the way here, the fact that he took me to his place means there's hope. So there's going to be no more excuses. I was rude. End of. I'll tell him that I'm sorry.

12.30 a.m.

Wow. Possibly the best making up ever. We're all loved-up again now. And I should really be sleeping, like he is, but something's bugging me. Stephen said I'd mocked Danielle in the players' lounge AND the salon. How could he know about the salon? Apart from Kellie, the only people who were there were Courtney, Lara and … ISABEL!

1 a.m.

I hate my life! It's like the worst episode of *EastEnders*. Only twice as miserable.

I know it's wrong but I checked Stephen's phone again. Had to take a deep breath first to prepare myself, then I clicked the text message icon on his BlackBerry. His messages weren't deleted this time. And I've seen the evidence: *I think we're made for each other. Love Courtney xxx*

What a bitch!

2.30 a.m.

I properly lost it. Literally launched his phone at him, barely missing his head – that woke him up all right.

"Of all the people – *Courtney*!" I screamed.

"She's been texting me like a mad woman. And I've told her a hundred times I'm not interested."

"Yeah, right," I barked. I'd had enough of playing the fool.

"Before yer accuse me – did yer see what I wrote back?"

"Don't need to. Been there, done that, with Robbie."

"I'm not Robbie."

"Do you think I don't know you've been deleting text messages? And as for your little poker excuse – bullshit! You must think I'm an idiot. You're *exactly* like Robbie. You're actually worse because at least he didn't pretend to be a good guy."

Stephen grabbed the phone off the bed, marched up to me and growled, "Now read my replies," as he pushed it into my hand. I've never seen anyone so angry.

I scrolled through his messages and read what he'd written back to her:

Ur a nice girl but I'm taken.

I'm not the one 4 u. But I'm sure he's out there somewhere.

I'm with Remy. You know that don't u?

Please stop phoning me. There's nothing more 2 say.

"She got my number that time Angus called her a cab. Started texting me from then."

"Why didn't you tell me?"

"I'm a big boy from Glasgow – I've dealt with much greater problems. Besides, yer can get a bit jealous and take things the wrong way – like when I look at a Post-it note."

"On a barmaid's *bum*."

"See what I mean? *And* you've been checking my text messages."

"Huh?"

"Yer said I'd deleted text messages. Well, people tend ter do that if their inboxes are full. And for the record, Remy, I *was* playing poker."

Maybe that was the time to say sorry. But I was still weighing up whether or not he was telling the truth.

"Yer know what?" he went on, still fuming. "A relationship is built on trust. So if yer can't trust me, maybe we should take a break."

I quickly apologized, said it was a misunderstanding and tried to change his mind, but it didn't work. So I took a cab home.

I am such an idiot! ☹

Thursday 12 March – 8.20 a.m.

Showered. Dressed. And ready to rip into Courtney!

11 a.m.

On a much-needed coffee break. I bought a triple-choc muffin too, as will probably need some extra energy – looks like I'll have to work through lunch now we don't have Courtney.

She got it as soon as I walked through the door this morning.

"I know all about your texts to Stephen, you cow! Now give me the keys. Get your things. And don't you ever step foot in this salon again."

"Sure. My *perleasure*," she said. And this wasn't the normal, apple-pie girl we were used to seeing. This was Courtney on bitch pills!

Lara and Isabel watched open-mouthed as she stormed over to the kitchenette to get her bag. She stormed back, took the keys out of it, and as she handed them over said, "You don't deserve to be a WAG. You don't even *like* football. And there's nothing Zoe Westwick can do to help *that*."

"Have you been reading my diary?"

"And I might have had a toddler haircut – but God knows what he sees in a farting, *paranoid* fatty like you!"

When Courtney walked out, Lara said, "If something seems too good to be true – it probably is."

"Yeah." I sighed. Can't believe she was playing me along like that. That's a new breed of WAG wannabe – the mutant kind.

Lara and Isabel have been stars. They both know beauticians who they think can replace Courtney, and they said I should go home early and they'd tell my clients I was ill. Lara even offered to lock up! But I decided to stay. Courtney might have lost me a boyfriend but I wasn't about to let her make me lose business as well.

7.45 P.M.

Home, shattered. So confused about what to do next with Stephen. But really sure about one thing: the dresses, shoes, bags and anything else that Robbie bought are getting packed away. RIGHT NOW. Dumping them in the morning.

<u>8.15 P.M.</u>

Not going to lie. It hurt to shove my leopard print Vivienne Westwood into a plastic bag but told myself I'll be able to buy even better on my own credit card one day.

Now lying on my bed wondering, if we're on a break, does that mean I have to wait for Stephen to call me, and I can't phone him? Because not speaking all day has been hard enough for me.

Will check what Malibu thinks. ☹

<u>9 P.M.</u>

That's it. The Bennets are cursed.

Called Mal, ready to sound off about Courtney, but she answered the phone crying.

"Ahh. Don't, Mal. It's just pre-wedding nerves," I told her.

"No, it's not," she answered. "The wedding's off."

It took ages to get it out of her, she was sobbing so much, but Mal has told Gary everything.

"I couldn't keep lying any more," she said. "I love him too much for that."

"What did he say?"

"He's so hurt, Rem. He's left the house and he wants me gone by the time he comes back."

"Wait there," I told her. "I'm coming round."

So I'm about to phone Dad so he can drive me there now.

11.30 P.M.

Malibu's in her old room, sleeping like a baby.

Dad was a legend tonight. End of. He was having dinner with Elizabeth and told her he'd have to go as soon as I said Mal was in trouble.

"And why exactly has the wedding been called off?" he asked a couple of times in the car on the way there.

"Um … not sure," I replied, because it's up to Malibu if she wants Dad to know.

We got there and helped pack as many of Mal's things as we could – enough to fill two huge suitcases – then drove home in silence. I opened the front door and watched her waddle in as Dad hauled each suitcase up to the front door.

Mum was in the kitchen waiting for her. "Oh Mal," she sighed.

I hoped at least one good thing would come out of it. "Come in for a cup of tea, Dad," I said.

"No, love. I'd better get off," he replied. ☹

Friday 13 March – 11.30 a.m.

Used my coffee break to go to Oxfam and gave them the stuff from Robbie. Best feeling ever!

Now just going to concentrate on two things:

1. Work.
2. Getting Malibu back on her feet.

As think I've blown it with Stephen.

Saturday 14 March – 8 a.m.

If anything, Malibu's got worse. I don't even want to go to work in case she needs me, but Mum says I have to and that she'll make sure Mal's all right.

Sunday 15 March – 3 a.m.

Spent the night by Malibu's side. She's been crying non-stop and wailing that her baby won't have a father – never seen anything like it. She's finally fallen asleep. Gutted for her.

10 a.m.

After a decent night's sleep, Malibu has developed titanium strength. This morning she walked into the kitchen and said she was tired of staying in her room and wanted to have breakfast with us.

"You know what," Mal said as Mum started scrambling eggs, "the only thing that matters is the baby is healthy. Everything else can work itself out. Or … probably not, in my case." Even though Mal followed her words with a laugh, I could tell that Mum, like me, didn't know if we were supposed to laugh too.

"It's OK, you know," Mal told us. "It's all about making the most of it. Cos I'm so over tears."

Now she's asked me to watch *Titanic* with her, "like the old days".

4 P.M.

Mal's incredible. Gary's had nothing to do with her since she left his house and instead of moaning about it, within ten minutes of *Titanic* starting she asked whether I'd like to be her birthing partner.

"Wow. I'd love to," I said.

And then she went into her birth plan.

"Ideally, I don't want any drugs. So I'm going to use a TENS machine."

"A what?"

Apparently a TENS machine will deliver electrical pulses to some pads that have to be placed on her back – for some reason that eases pain.

"Will it work for a broken heart?" I sighed.

"Let's make that two," she answered.

"We're a right pair. All that talk about the husbands we

were going to have and the houses we'd love to live in, and we're both here – single, living with Mum."

"You've still got a chance. So bloody get off your ass and phone Stephen."

"But he said he wants a break."

"You're not going to take any notice of that, are you? Have you listened to anything I've taught you over the years? Call him. Don't give up. *Ever.*"

So… Here goes…

4.30 P.M.

"Hi. It's Remy. How are you?"

Stephen was monosyllabic at first. "Fine."

"And Angus?"

"Good."

"Saw you scored another goal yesterday. Congrats."

"Ta."

"I miss you," I blurted out. "Can we please meet tomorrow? Just for a chat."

"Aw, Boss Lady," he said. "What took yer so long?"

We arranged to meet after work. It doesn't mean we're back together. And there's still a lot of humble pie for me to eat, but in the meantime – woo-hoo!

6 P.M.

Intend to be the best birthing partner on the planet, so

been online searching for books. Decided to order one called *Lamaze Breathing Techniques*. (It has four stars.)

Bring it on!

Monday 16 March – 8.25 a.m.

Showered.
Make-up: Glam.
Hair: Glam.
Dressed: Double-glam.
Mind: Set on winning back my man!

10 a.m.

Yippee! The Tah-dah! loyalty cards have arrived. They look the business.

Also seeing two possible replacements for Courtney today.

11.20 a.m.

"Have you spoken to him yet?" This is how Kellie has started every phone call with me since I broke up with Stephen. This time I was happy to report, "Yep. Meeting him later."

"Yay! What a result."

Our conversations have been a lot shorter lately. I think we've both been trying to avoid bringing up the humongous white elephant in the room, but for some reason today I couldn't hold it in any more.

"So, how's it going with *David Joseph*?"

I didn't mean it to sound as bitchy as it ended up coming out.

"Look," said Kel, "I know this is going to come across as two-faced, after all I said about WAGs, but not only is he hotter than Jack – he's tons more exciting than him as well."

"But what are you gonna do about Jack?"

"Um… As of twenty minutes ago, we're on a break."

"Kel," I sighed. "Who d'you think you are – Stephen?"

3.30 P.M.

Met the first possible Courtney replacement at two – Lara told her to come in. Liked her a lot. Her name's Emily Winterflood and her specialities are nail art and vajazzles!

The next one, Charlie Sykes, came at three. Isabel used to work at a salon called Allure with her. She said I'd be impressed – and I am. Charlie's confident without being arrogant and says she's having difficulties with one of the girls at the salon so would love to start as soon as. Hmm… #Decisions

7.05 P.M.

Locking up and then going to meet Stephen. So–oo nervous.

Aaa–aaaaaargh!

We met somewhere neutral. A small restaurant in Marylebone called Villandry. And I'm sure the food tastes as good as it looks but I didn't get to eat it.

Stephen had got there before me, so the waitress showed me to the table, and seeing him again – his tousled brown hair and luscious lips – made my heart beat off the chart.

"You look beautiful," he said.

Thought certain things would stop once I became an adult but, no, I was still blushing like a first year in infant school.

"No Angus?" I asked.

"Naw. He offered, but I told him to stay home."

"Jeez, I hope he can cope."

"Aye, so do I."

It would have been nice to natter like that, but it would have been avoiding what needed to be said. And I was fed up with dodging facts. So I jumped straight in after the waitress took our order and left.

"OK. I'll start," I said. "This break has given me a chance to think things through, and you're right, a relationship is built on trust. And I think I would have trusted you normally. To be honest, I don't think it had anything to do with you. It was to do with Robbie and what he'd done."

"But I'm nothing like him. Yer should have taken a second to remember that."

"I know. But I didn't take enough time to get over him. Well, not *him* – what he'd done. I was still hurting, and I let it seep over into our relationship. I'm sorry. And I won't let it happen again."

"Yer turned into someone I didn't recognize. And if we do stay together, Remy, I want back the girl I fell in love with in Turkey."

Love?

"Hang on a minute, did you just say … love?" I had to check.

"Aye. What's wrong with that?" he asked when I started to giggle.

"Nothing. It's just I love you too, ya big … haggis."

"Aww, is that right?" he said, leaning towards me.

"Yes. Very, very, *very* right." I moved my head forward to meet his. We started kissing just as the waitress arrived with our starters.

"If yer don't mind, I think we'd like to get the bill," Stephen told her, giving me a knowing smile.

We went back to his and everything was perfect, but I knew there was one more thing left to discuss. Because him loving me is great and all that, but I had to check that he'd fallen for the real Remy, and that meant I had a few confessions to make.

Star Wars disappointed him. Boxing, he said he sort of knew because I kept calling one of the boxers Floyd

MOweather, instead of MAYweather. But the Kings of Leon… That hurt.

"You mean, you don't like them *very* much?"

"No. I mean … they suck."

"Naw way. You're winding me up."

"I'm serious, I can think of at least thirty better people off the top of my head."

"Go on then."

"David Guetta—"

"Woah. Remind me what instrument he plays."

"The decks of course. Black Eyed Peas—"

"Pah!"

"Rihanna—"

"Cannae sing."

"Tinie Tempah—"

"Aw naw. This is gonna be a deal-breaker, I can tell," he said with a big grin on his face.

I challenged him to a sound clash, so we got out our iPods. It took nineteen songs before we got to one that we both liked: Calvin Harris' "I'm Not Alone".

"Choooon!" I cried when it came on.

"Aye, he's a good Scottish lad."

And as we were clearing the slate, there was just one more thing I needed to know: "Baby, what do you think about Isabel?"

"Isabel – who's that?"

"The girl who works in my salon. The Spanish one. And it's fine for you to say she's pretty, I won't mind."

"Aw, *her*. She's very pretty, aye. But she's not you."

How can I not love him? ☺

<u>Tuesday 17 March – 7.30 a.m.</u>

Showered? Check! Dressed? Check! Keys to salon? Check! A sleeping man who loves me? Double-check!!

<u>Saturday 21 March – 10 p.m.</u>

Malibu's waters have broken! Twelve days early! Thank God I've spent every spare minute reading up on labour. Her contractions haven't started yet and the general advice is to wait until they do before going to the hospital. But that's for normal babies. If this little Bennet is anything like its mother, it probably tore up the rule book at conception! Now, must put what I've learnt into practice and be a v. together birthing partner.

TENS machine? Check!

Lamaze Breathing Techniques? Check!

Phone Dad? Check!

And Mum's just shouted that the cab's arrived (she's coming with us). So, let's go.

Aa–aaaaaaargh!

<u>Sunday 22 March – 2.30 p.m.</u>

Thirteen long hours. Tons of inhaled gas and air (and that's just by me). A TENS machine chucked across the room for not providing enough pain relief. Or, to quote Malibu, it was "doing fuck all!" (Contractions were ten minutes apart at that point.) I sprayed her face with water, held her hand, did my best to talk her through the breathing; but it was painful to watch, let alone go through. Malibu says it's the hardest thing she's ever done by a long shot, but so–oo blooming worth it because all eight pounds, three ounces of my little nephew are absolutely beautiful. ☺

It was an honour to be the second person to hold him, but it was just as satisfying to pass him to Mum and then watch her pass him to Dad. Yes, they were actually in the same room as each other!

"Look at the little munchkin," Dad said.

"Isn't he beautiful," Mum agreed, and they stood there cooing at him – all wrongs forgiven (maybe) but most definitely forgotten. Dad even took us home.

Phoned Stephen to tell him the good news just as we were leaving the hospital. He was getting ready for his game this afternoon.

"That's fantastic. We'll have to get the wee fella a football kit," he said.

"Nah. With all due respect, I think he's gonna be prime minister."

Now about to send out some texts. Well, actually two. A group one saying: *Am now a proud auntie to a little nephew. Woo-hoo!* And a second, much more sensitive one, to Gary. The little munchkin has tightly curled black hair and big brown eyes – the opposite of Malibu and Lance – so even a thicko at Science like me could work it out.

I wrote: *Think it's only right 4 u 2 know that u have a son. Born this morning. He's beautiful. Remy x*

Then I decided to add something that Malibu said as she held the baby in her arms: *He looks just like u.*

Exhausted. Going to sleep.

<u>6 P.M.</u>

Wow. Got three hours' kip and I'm full of beans, maybe because I can't stop smiling about being an auntie. And I know exactly what kind of auntie I'm going to be too. A cool one that my nephew can come and talk to about cigarettes, girls, sex, etc.

Yay! The doorbell has just rung. That will be Dad. We're going to bring Mal and my baby nephew home from hospital. ☺

<u>8 P.M.</u>

"Can I come too?" Mum called out to Dad as I got into his car.

"Yeah… Course you can," Dad replied. And that was all Mum needed to hear to say goodbye to Alan and jump in with us.

We were so excited about seeing the baby again that

we got all the way to the maternity ward before realizing we'd forgotten to bring the baby's seat in from the car.

"The baby's not allowed to leave the hospital without one," the nurse on duty told us.

Doh! "It's OK, I'll go," I volunteered. Going back to the car was a good opportunity for me to check my texts one last time, because I'd had tons of replies from my friends but received nothing from the person who mattered the most: Gary. And it has stayed that way. ☹

Mal and the baby have gone to her room to sleep, and Dad has offered to drop me at Stephen's. Been in such a baby bubble that I have no idea how his match turned out, but I'm assuming he scored because I have a text from Kellie that says: *Your man's gangsta!*

10 P.M.

When we pulled up outside Stephen's, I told Dad, "You're the best. And we're so lucky to have you." Was feeling proper sorry for him because on the way I'd asked how it was going with Elizabeth and he'd sighed, then said, "She's a good woman, Remy. But she's not your mum." ☹

Stephen opened the front door, sporting his latest accessory: a big black eye!

"What happened?" I gasped.

"Aw, nothing. Just a little disagreement with Robbie."

"What?!"

Stephen was v. sheepish about it, so Angus did most

of the filling in. Robbie got upset when Stephen took a free kick, which unfortunately he missed. Robbie then said, "That's why you're only fit for my leftovers." Stephen shrugged it off until half-time, when he socked Robbie one as they were making their way into the tunnel.

"And Remy, Stevie's eye is nothing compared with the little prick's," said Angus, making his Scottish accent even thicker. "We're from Glasgee, man."

The manager substituted the pair of them. That meant they couldn't start the second half and he's called them both in for a meeting tomorrow.

"Oh no," I groaned.

"It's OK. I'll probably just get a fine," Stephen told me.

"Hmm. Well, I'll have to give that eye some special medicine."

"Oh yeah – what's that?"

"Something called 'Kiss it better'."

"Aw, that sounds good," he replied. So I intend to spoil him for the rest of the night.

Monday 23 March – 8.55 a.m.

Stephen and Robbie's fight made the papers! It was Stephen's agent that told us. He phoned at early o'clock and woke us up.

"Who's that?" I asked Stephen sleepily.

"Och, God knows."

He mustered up enough energy to stretch his arm

out to his BlackBerry, sitting on the bedside table, and answered it.

"Hello Harry… Yeah, yeah, I know." He sounded remorseful at first and then got angry. "What?" He leapt out of bed, stormed over to his laptop on top of the drawers, typed furiously and then said, "Oh–hhh shit."

Harry started to bark instructions down the phone.

"Yeah, yeah OK," Stephen said. "I'll show it to her now and call you back." He ended the call. "Remy, yer need to see this."

I walked over and that's when I saw it splashed across the *Sun*: MY GIRL. With a pic of Robbie and Stephen, mid punch-up, underneath. Will never believe something I read in a paper again after seeing this article. It was spouting crap about a girl who had "allegedly" had a secret affair with Stephen, and caused a rift that might break up the team. To make it worse, the footnote said: If you know the identity of the mystery girl, please call.

"Shit in hell."

"I'll sort it, I promise," Stephen told me. "I'll even do a quick interview if I need to. Set the record straight."

Hope so. Because every time someone looked at me on my way in to the salon this morning, I felt like shouting: I'M INNOCENT. ☺

1.20 P.M.

OMG. Went out to get a sandwich for lunch and on my

200

way back, a man jumped out of a Ford Focus parked outside the salon. He had a huge camera in his hand, and
began to snap photos of me!

I think this means I've been paparazzied!

<u>7.30 P.M.</u>

Spoke to Stephen all the way home. Grumbled about
being papped but was too embarrassed to admit that
it also felt quite exciting. Me – Remy Louise Bennet
– being treated like a superstar. That's cra–aazy! Was
actually slightly gutted when Paparazzi Man wasn't outside when I left – he must have found a real celebrity to
photograph.

"It probably won't appear anywhere, OK? So try not to
fret about it."

"OK. I'll *try*."

"And Harry's set up an interview for me tomorrow. *I'll
nip it in the bud, geezer*," he said, putting on his agent's
Cockney voice.

Right, time to get on with the reason I've decided to
come home instead of going to Stephen's: my baby nephew
is due a big hug. ☺

<u>8 P.M.</u>

Yes! Yes! Yes! Gary came over.

I was in Mal's room at the time, singing "Three Blind

Mice" to the bubba, when the doorbell rang.

"Who's that?" Malibu wondered.

"I dunno," I said with a shrug.

When Mum knocked on her door and told her it was Gary, her eyes nearly jumped out of her skull. I, on the other hand, looked double, triple guilty.

"Did you tell him about the baby?" she hissed at me.

I didn't want her to go mad again – we'd made progress since my last episode of Big-mouth Syndrome – so for a split second I thought about denying it; but this was something I was proud of.

"Yes," I admitted, and was ready to explain but didn't need to because Mal threw her arms around me and said, "Thanks, sis." Felt warm tears on my cheek just before she pulled away. "Right, I look like shit. Um… One minute," she called out. Off came the scrunchie, down came the hair, and she rubbed off the spot of baby vomit on her shoulder. "You can come in now."

Twenty seconds later, in walked Gary. I will never forget the look on his face when he saw his baby boy. My little nephew has brought pure joy to this house, and I can't wait to tell him that one day.

Methinks I may have to buy that chief bridesmaid dress after all. ☺

Tuesday 24 March – 8.55 a.m.

Almost nine o'clock and I'm still at home. Have no choice.

I had seven missed calls from Dad when I came out of the shower. Dad wouldn't chase me like that unless it was pretty urgent, so I called him.

"Dad. Are you OK?" I asked.

"Yes… Er… No… Well, sort of. Are you home?"

"Yes."

"Good. I'm outside. Can I come in?"

Outside? Wow. Thought it must be something proper bad for him to turn up so early in the morning.

He was standing at the door by the time I opened it, with a rolled-up newspaper in his hand. Dad, the calmest man on earth, was in a right old panic. I glanced at the newspaper he was holding. "Oh, has Stephen done the story?" I said, relieved. "It's nothing to worry about, Dad. He said it was best to clear things up."

"Um… Well… I think something must have gone wrong."

I frowned. "Why?"

Dad unrolled the paper and showed me its front page:

The Girl Who's Divided a Team!

And there I was, walking into the salon. That pap from yesterday!

Haven't fully read the story yet, because my phone keeps ringing. First with a v. sorry Stephen saying that Harry Burton, his agent, will call me to try and sort things out. Then Harry himself.

"I say we gotta make the most of this, doll."

"Huh?"

"You're a pretty girl. You just bin seen by about six million people. We could make ya the new Coleen Rooney."

Oh Lawd.

Acknowledgements

With thanks to:
KT Forster
Helen McAleer
Gill Evans
Emma Lidbury
Annalie Grainger
Claire Sandeman
Jo Humphreys-Davies and the marketing team
Kate Beal
Sean Moss
Maria Soler Canton
Jas Chana and everyone at Mobcast
Mark Hodgson and BlackBerry
Ruth Harrison and The Reading Agency
Caroline Odland
Tim Holloway

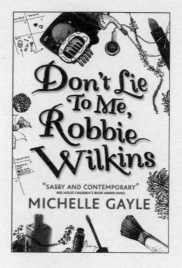

OMG! My bum looks *huge* in this LBD!

Minutes away from a date with Robbie Wilkins.
Him: The buffest Premiership footballer around.
Me: Now officially an elephant. ☺

I can't believe I snogged him on my
17th-and-a-half birthday! (He's a proper catch.)

Kellie says I should tell him my salon business
plans: not just BEAUTIFUL but ambitious too. ☺

This is gonna be an amaaaaaazing year…